Almost

Lori Bell

Cover photograph by Vecteezy

Printed by Kindle Direct Publishing

ISBN 9798873739899

DEDICATION

To find what you've never had, you have to do what you've never done. (Thomas Jefferson)

Chapter 1

She was numb, incapable of feeling any emotion that threatened to surface. Useless and broken. The tragic past few days of her life had ripped out her soul, and everything in her orbit had blurred. Maureen Ryan was surrounded by people, practically everyone she had ever crossed paths with in her forty-eight years of life. She graciously listened to their words, but she had not really heard anything. She accepted more food than she had ever seen at once in the kitchen of her home, yet she hadn't eaten a bite.

She wore a sleeveless, straight-cut, black dress that ended just above the knee. It was October in the Midwest, where the temperatures fluctuated from chilly to warm in a single day. By nightfall, she needed a layer, but the best she could do right now was cross her arms over her chest as she stood in the cool air on the outside deck of her home that overlooked the backyard. She escaped the noise inside to have a minute to herself. She didn't want to feel another hug or hear additional words of support and encouragement. If one more person told her, *I'm here if you need anything,* she was going to unravel.

She heard the door open and close behind her, but she never turned around. A second later, she felt the warmth of a blanket draped over her shoulders and down the length of her back.

"Reen," Her lifelong friend, Quinn Palmer, comforted her with a familiar fleece blanket from inside, the one that was typically folded over the back of the recliner in Maureen's living room. "Take this. Wrap it around you, if you are going to stay out here half naked."

Maureen smirked a little in response. No words were necessary between two people who shared a solid friendship throughout four decades of ups and downs. This, for Maureen, was going to be documented in her book of life as the worst thing that ever happened to her. This was rock bottom.

The two of them stood near the railing of the deck's edge. Quinn, who was called *Palmer* all her life, wrapped one arm around her dearest friend. Palmer was a 5'9" brunette, and Maureen was a tad shorter at 5'7," and blonder. Through the layer of the blanket, Palmer could feel her body trembling.

"I am here for you," Palmer choked on a sob, but Maureen appeared unaffected. "Listen to me. Reen? Please." Palmer gently turned Maureen's body to face her own. "I am not going to pretend to completely understand your pain, but I am here to feel it with you. Just feel it. Okay? It's the only healthy way to—"

"Don't." Maureen stopped her. "Do not tell me that I will heal." The pain in her quivering voice was heart-wrenching. "There is no way, being completely whole again after something like this, will ever be possible." Maureen shook her head and looked away, but Palmer already saw the tears welling up in her eyes. "I am so done with these tears. I am all cried out. I cannot do it anymore."

Palmer allowed her own tears to freefall. "I wish I could take it all away for you, rewind time, and keep it from happening."

"You're telling me. I've replayed this over and over again in my mind, like it's on some kind of relentless reel."

"You need rest," Palmer suggested, cautiously, because she already knew Maureen wasn't eating much and likely could not be forced to get some sleep either. She saw exhaustion in her eyes, but not solely from lack of sleep. She wore the face of a woman who was broken. Life's hardship had beaten her down. Those age earned stubborn lines around her sad eyes had deepened.

"Is everyone still here?" Maureen glanced at the back windows of the house, attempting to see if there were too many people still moving around in there, or lingering on her furniture. She had never really been one for having company over. Palmer was an exception.

"Mostly, yeah. The ones, who did leave, I told them that you needed a minute and not to bother you for a goodbye."

Maureen laughed a little. It was the first time she had done so in days. And then she uttered, "My personal badass."

Palmer proudly and purposely straightened her posture. "I look out for my own."

"Then help me make a b-line straight for my bedroom when we go back inside. I just want to shut the world out."

"You might find Archer doing the same thing."

"What?" Maureen imagined her husband still sitting beside their family and friends inside, consumed with devastation, but reiterating how proud he was of his only son. Yet so regretful that his life had come to an abrupt and tragic end. He had been saying the same thing to her for days, while Maureen was handling her devastation altogether differently. She was detached.

"I saw him go upstairs and into Isaac's room. I gave him some time before I knocked and went in." Maureen held her breath. She closed her son's bedroom door days ago, and neither of them had been able to go in there since. It instantly angered her that her husband had gone in first, or at all. She didn't know why, perhaps it just felt too sacred. She wanted everything left as it was. Untouched. "Archer had Isaac's phone. He was upset that he could not figure out the passcode."

"What does that matter right now?"

"It matters to him, Reen. Archer lost his son, too."

Maureen stayed silent. She didn't know what to feel. She had no idea how to navigate through this sudden and unbearable loss. Her entire life. Her purpose for the last 14 years was gone. Forever.

Palmer stood in the background as she watched everyone slowly begin to filter out of the Ryan's home. There were more tears and additional words of encouragement from some, and silence from others. Because what do you say at a time like this that hasn't already been said? She was worried about Maureen.

She was stoic. Losing her boy had hardened her. Through the shock and the sadness, it was her coping mechanism to shut down. Palmer was cautiously aware of this gradually worsening because Isaac Ryan was gone.

When she closed the door behind her, Palmer was there, gripping her shoulders. "Where the hell is Archer?" Maureen immediately lashed out.

"I saw him saying goodbye to the neighbors before he slipped away."

"Isaac's room again?"

Palmer shook her head. "No, yours."

Maureen glanced at the open staircase that led to the bedrooms, but she did not move.

"I should go. You two need this time." Palmer suggested.

Maureen reached for her. "I don't know what I need anymore." She glanced at the framed pictures on the fireplace mantel. "The boy who called me mom is gone. He was my one and only. How do I ever begin again after that?"

Palmer pulled her close, Maureen held onto her for dear life, and then she heard Palmer's words close to her ear. "You just try your best to live. It's all you can do."

Chapter 2

Maureen heard Archer moving around in their bedroom. He spun around when she opened the door, as if he was caught off guard. Archer was the stereotypical tall, dark, and handsome male. He was 50 years old, but he was still as youthful as he was two decades ago. He had changed out of his dark suit that he wore to the funeral, and was now wearing jeans, a T-shirt, and tennis shoes. They never wore shoes in the house until the moment they were going out the door. She spotted their largest suitcase open on the foot-end of the bed. He turned away from her to firmly press down on the folded clothing inside with both of his hands, and then he zipped it closed.

"What is going on here?"

Her husband averted his eyes momentarily before he spoke. "I can't do this. I can't stay here. It will never be the same without Isaac." Maureen saw the tears well up in his eyes.

"So you want to move? Meanwhile, you're what? Staying at a hotel? And why was I not included in this decision?"

Archer avoided giving her a direct answer.

"I'm moving out, Reen. There's nothing left. We both know that our son was keeping us together."

She didn't want to talk about this now. Not on the day they buried their child. Everything was happening all at once. Her son was gone. Her husband was leaving her. She never expected life to be fair, but all of this thrown at her now was beyond incomprehensible.

A part of her wanted to say nothing, and just let him go. Giving up felt like her best option. Instead, she spoke to him.

"We can go to counseling. I know I am going to need professional help to navigate through this grief, because I am well aware of how I cannot think straight or process anything. Archer, don't react too soon. Now is not the time to make rash decisions about anything in our lives."

"I need time… and space," he responded as if he didn't hear a word she had said. "I can't accept or heal or whatever it is I'm supposed to do, as long as I am under this roof. This house was our home as a family, and now that is gone. I feel empty here."

"You never asked me if I wanted to lock up this house and never look back."

"You haven't exactly been reachable, Reen."

"My son died. No, my son ended his life. He sold himself short after only 14 years." Maureen inhaled a deep breath to keep her composure. "And the worst part of all is I have no idea why." Archer looked away. Men were supposed to be tough, the stronger species, but when it came down to handling the worst, they fell apart. Archer's face was tear-soaked, and Maureen didn't stop for a second to comfort him, to grieve alongside her husband. "I am so angry with him, but I have forced myself not to express that. I am unbelievably sad, but sick and tired of crying. I want to go back out to that cemetery and lay down beside him, because I feel just as lifeless as that boy. And now, here you are… you're leaving me, too."

"He was also my son." Archer choked on those words through his tears. "You seem to have forgotten that. I want him back more than anything in this world. Now, all I can do is go into his bedroom and press his clothes to my face, so I do not forget how he smelled. I have never felt so lost in my life, and if I am going to survive this, I have to start over anywhere but here."

What he said triggered her memory of when Palmer mentioned that Archer was trying to get into Isaac's cell phone.

"I don't want you to take anything from his room. Not yet. I am not ready to part with his belongings." Archer stayed silent. "I want his phone to stay here."

She recognized that look on his face. He was uncomfortable because he was caught. "You have it, don't you?"

He nodded. "I don't know the passcode."

"Why is that so important right now?"

Archer refrained from answering her.

"Leave Isaac's phone here," she said again.

He reached into the back pocket of his denim, and then he reluctantly set the phone down on their bed behind him. A moment later, he hoisted the suitcase by its handle, and walked past her. "I will be back for the rest of my things some other time."

There was a cold, distant vibe between them. The connection they once shared was severed. And Maureen couldn't explain that any differently than she could her son's choice to leave this world, and her, behind.

The only thing she knew for sure was she had lost her fight. Her reservoir of energy to beg and plead, or bargain, was empty. *Just go,* she thought. *I don't even care anymore.*

Maureen walked around that big empty house in the dark with only the illumination of the streetlights shining through the open window blinds, which she never bothered to close.

She wondered if she, too, could walk away from this home. Being there always felt like a step back in time. The first time she saw that historic Victorian home on 2.3 acres, she wanted it to be hers. Theirs. She was about to give birth to a baby boy. She was so certain that, with Isaac, she and Archer would be a family forever. She never expected what happened in that house. No one ever imagined the worst.

The grand foyer had an open staircase, inlaid wood flooring, and pocket doors to enter the dining room. A decorative arched entry led to a sun-filled living room, and another set of pocket doors led to the family room. The kitchen was accented with white cabinets, quartz countertops, tile backsplash, a viking cooktop and double ovens. The master bedroom and four additional bedrooms were on the second floor.

Maureen felt so small in all that space now.

She still had not changed out of her black dress, the one she was certain she would never wear again. It would be branded in her mind as her funeral dress, worn the day she said a final, god-awful goodbye to her only child. Just another memory she wished to forget.

From the outside looking in, no one would ever believe Maureen Ryan's life had been complicated and challenging. She was familiar with putting on a brave face since she was a child. At only three years old, Maureen was orphaned. Until she was nine years old, she had been tossed in and out of foster homes, never truly feeling as if she belonged anywhere. That changed in the fourth grade when Palmer befriended her, and Palmer's parents took her in as their own.

Maureen stood behind the recliner chair in her living room and placed her open palms on the gray fleece blanket, folded in half and hanging there. She felt the weight of knowing that all she had was Palmer. Everyone else had left her. Yet again.

Palmer tried the door handle after knocking and waiting outside on the front porch. She stepped inside and found a quiet house. She momentarily wondered if they were still asleep, but the open blinds and unlocked door made her think otherwise. Then, she saw Maureen curled up, on the far end of the sectional, partially covered with a blanket, still wearing yesterday's dress. That was warranted. She had just lost her son. She didn't feel like eating, showering, changing clothes, or apparently even sharing a bed with her husband. At this point, Palmer debated waking her. If she tiptoed her way out the front door, Maureen could continue to rest.

"You brought coffee," Maureen spoke with her eyes still closed, and Palmer smiled. In her hands she held a tray of two large cups with flat sipper lids, and a bag of asiago bagels with cream cheese. Archer wasn't a coffee drinker, but she brought enough bagels, just in case he was around. It was still too soon for either of them to go back to work.

"Hey... I was standing here debating if I should leave your breakfast on the table and let you sleep for a while."

"It doesn't matter. It's not restful sleep," Maureen spoke as she sat up on the end of the sofa, trying to be somewhat graceful in a dress. Her shoulder-length blonde hair was matted, and the day-old makeup needed to be washed off her face. Palmer wasn't judging her by any means. The two of them had been through it all together, their best and their lowest. She only wanted to take care of her now, to hold her up through this awful loss.

"Sleeping in your bed might help?" Palmer handed Maureen a coffee, and she was relieved to see her eagerly accept it. Next, she would attempt to force feed her a bagel.

"Archer left," was all Maureen said with an unaltered expression.

"For work? Maybe he needs to keep his mind busy." Everyone handled their grief differently, but Palmer refrained from saying as much, because all this talk of death and grief was taking its toll.

Maureen shook her head. "After everyone left yesterday, he was in our bedroom packing. He said he can't do this anymore. He doesn't want to live in this house without our son. That decision also includes no longer wanting to be with me." Palmer watched Maureen all but shrug off the idea of her marriage dissolving.

"Did you see this coming?" Palmer had so much else she wanted to say.

"What I never, in my worst nightmare, saw coming was my son's suicide. Everything else pales in comparison. I'm sorry if that makes me seem heartless. It's just how I feel. And if Archer wants out, I don't have the energy to fight for him."

Palmer refrained from encouraging her to save her marriage. "Let's eat these bagels. I brought your favorite." She held up the bag to entice her, and then turned toward the kitchen.

"I should get out of this dress."

"You should also stand in a hot shower for a long while, but first, you need to eat."

Palmer watched Maureen devour half the bagel, after smothering it with cream cheese, and she also finished her coffee.

"Thank you for eating."

"I didn't want to be rude," Maureen gave her a silly excuse and a lopsided grin.

"There's a whole refrigerator full of gifted food, so don't be rude. Eat up."

They laughed.

"What am I going to do with all that? Especially with Archer gone, so much food will go to waste."

"Do you really think he's gone for good?"

"Palmer, all my life, everyone has left. Until you... and your wonderful parents."

"*Our* parents," Palmer corrected her. "I still stand by the truth that they love you more than me."

Maureen rolled her eyes.

"You're stuck with us."

"I know that," Maureen responded. "When I needed something of my own, you and your family allowed me to feel as if I belonged. But it wasn't until Isaac was born that I no longer felt as if I was almost there. I was home, I was finally fulfilled. Being almost enough was so far from my thoughts the last 14 years. And now, here I am, back to feeling like my life, my happiness, my complete fulfillment, will always be out of reach."

"Isaac will remain a part of you. You are still his mother, the one person who will keep his memory alive in your heart."

"That's what they say, but really? How will that ever take the place of having him here, raising him, and watching him find himself in this world?"

Palmer shook her head, as if to agree that it wouldn't.

Chapter 3

Palmer's parents were the closest thing to a mom and dad Maureen ever had in her life. They were in their early eighties now, still living on a farm in the midwestern town of Highland, Illinois. Maureen drove the backroads, through the flat countryside from her own house to theirs. It was only a few miles. The farm was set deeper into the country than Maureen's house, which was located on the edge of the countryside in a neighborhood. The farmland was still fertile, but Jon and Atta Palmer were no longer able to be at the helm, caring for or managing it. Jon, however, still tinkered in the barns and sat behind the wheel of a tractor just to give himself a purpose. And that's exactly what Maureen saw him doing, driving in the open field, as she stepped out of her vehicle. She raised her arm in the air and waved before she stepped onto the wrap-around porch, where Atta was calling her name from the high-back rocking chair. "Reen, honey. Come sit down by me."

There was genuine sympathy in her eyes, and Maureen tried not to return her sad stare. She didn't want anyone's worry or concern. She wasn't sure why she had come there. She knew this loss was also slowly killing the two people who were doting grandparents to her child. Maureen carefully sat down on the chair beside Atta. She told herself to remain in control, because if she relaxed her body now, she would fall apart. Truthfully, she had always lived like that; it was the only way she knew how to go on living. When she let her defenses down, she struggled to find her way back. And this time, after what life had thrown at her, she knew she would go to pieces, and the pieces would be blown away.

Father Time hadn't been unkind to Atta. She had the whitest, fullest, head of healthy hair still. Her shoulders were narrow, and her legs were long. That's where Palmer got her 5'9" frame. She wore a powder blue sweatsuit with a white puffer vest for an additional layer. The wide-open air was always gustier out there on the farm. The ankle high white Ugg boots on her feet made Maureen smile. She was the most stylish farmer's wife.

They shared silence, because that's what Atta did. As far back as nine years old, Maureen could remember the comfort of this woman holding space for her. She was always willing to walk alongside her without judgement, and she especially never tried to fix anything or impact the outcome. She only offered unconditional support.

"Are you waiting for Jon Boy to make his way inside for the day?" Maureen never called the man, who had a hand in raising her, dad. And she was the only one who got away with calling him Jon Boy. It was an endearing way to address him, and it fit because he had always been a sensitive soul, with soft edges... like a boy.

"I am," Atta nodded. "He overdoes it, I tell you. I'll actually be glad to see winter come to slow him down some."

Maureen no longer cared about which season came or went. As far as she felt now, the dead of winter had settled in her soul. Permanently.

"I didn't know where else to go," Maureen stated, staring at the open land.

"You never need an excuse to come home," Atta tried to smile through the tears welling up in her eyes. "I just wish our boy had not been so troubled."

Maureen jerked her head toward Atta. "But he wasn't. I mean, if there were ever signs, he hid them. Something had to have happened for his reaction to be so dire. We may never know, and that just might bury me."

"There was sadness, Reen. There was too much time spent alone."

"He was a teenager, who could sometimes be moody, and he liked his space." Was she making excuses for him? Did others see something out of the ordinary or alarming in her son that she, his own mother, missed?

Atta nodded. "No use in carrying guilt. Isaac was his own person. No one could force him to do anything, nor change his mind once it was made up."

Maureen smiled a little. "Strong willed. I always thought that would get him far in life."

"No matter the unbearable pain now, we would not have traded those 14 years with that wonderful child."

"Thank you," Maureen's gratitude was genuine.

"We know that Archer left," Atta shared, somewhat cautiously. "Quinn told us." Palmer's birth-given name was Quinn, and of course her parents never got on the bandwagon to call her Palmer.

Maureen shrugged. "At least he knows what will make him happier."

"Don't excuse his behavior. He's a coward."

"You've never liked him," Maureen noted with a smirk.

"What I didn't like was the control he had over you."

"I learned to pick my battles, Atta."

"A woman only has so much fight left in her once she's been worn down."

Maureen turned her body to face the wise woman who she hoped had formed her as a person the last four decades of her life. She wanted some of that collective wisdom and clarity. She wanted to believe that life's joy outweighed the pain and made it all worth it. But she wasn't so sure anymore.

"I will survive Archer leaving me. It's Isaac. I will never recover from losing him."

"It feels that way now. It's all so raw, the wound is still open."

"So just allow it to scab over and I'll eventually toughen up?" Maureen's tone was snarky.

"No," Atta shook her head slowly. "Nothing is ever good at surface level. You must dig deep, feel the pain, and eventually overcome it. I still see the 9-year-old child in you. The one who would say, "I'm fine," no matter what she was feeling, or how bad something hurt."

Maureen looked away.

"Before you arrived in our lives, a few years before that day when Quinn brought you home from school and told us that you needed a safe place to stay, a home, I left this farm and my family."

Palmer confided in Maureen, long ago, that her mother had gone away for several months, when she was six years old, and it was never talked about why. At this moment, Maureen felt uncomfortable knowing that Atta appeared to want to share something off-limits with her, like that well-kept secret.

"I couldn't have more children after my Quinn. We tried, but it wasn't to be. I knew how badly Jon wanted boys to work on this farm and carry on his legacy. We didn't talk about it much. We just carried on." Maureen watched Atta pause, as if the memory of something was still haunting after all these years. "Late, one night, after Quinn had gone to sleep, I took a walk on the grounds. Jon was in the main barn, or so I had thought. I heard activity in one of our smaller sheds, so I looked inside. Jon was in there, and another woman was with him. I stood there and watched the two of them in the throes of forbidden passion. He took her from behind. That's not something we ever did. Never mind I said that."

Maureen tried to hide her shock. "Atta... did you leave him after that night?"

She shook her head. "Not right away, no. I never spoke of it. I just gradually distanced myself from my husband. It was many months later when he told me that he had a confession to make. He had gotten another woman pregnant. He begged me to understand that he didn't want her, he only wanted the child she was carrying. His son."

Palmer didn't have a sibling. Jon and Atta had been married for 57 years. Everything about this story did not make any sense to Maureen. Atta could see the questions in her eyes, and she continued.

"I forbade it. He wasn't going to embarrass me like that or tarnish our family's image. I knew who the woman was, and let me tell you, it was never a sure thing that the child she claimed to be carrying was Jon's. That floozy got around." Maureen stifled her laughter, because this was not funny. What was comical to her was she had never heard Atta speak ill of anyone. Clearly, a woman scorned shouldn't be underestimated.

"I drove to town that night. I saw her vehicle at Rail Shake." That was the historical building, along a stretch of railroad tracks in Highland. It was built in 1856, and originally housed a hotel but served as a tavern for a majority of the years. For the past two decades, it was a restaurant and bar. "She was a bar fly there, always serving drinks and bouncing on laps." Again, Maureen's eyes widened by Atta's word choice.

"Did you confront her?" Maureen could not imagine that scene. Everything she was hearing was contradictory of Atta's character.

"No, but I did find her car in the parking lot. Growing up with brothers, I knew what I was doing. I cut her brakes. And I left." Atta reacted to the shock on Maureen's face. "I wanted her out of our lives."

"Atta… what happened? Did she die?" she paused. "And the baby?"

"She was intoxicated when she left the tavern that night. She ran her car off the road. Yes, she died. There was no baby. She lied to Jon about that. Perhaps she thought he would leave his family for her?"

"This is a lot to process," Maureen realized for the first time in several days she was not thinking about her loss and suffocating from the grief. "Why did you choose to share this with me? I mean, that's a secret you probably should have taken to your grave." She moved her eyes to the farmland. "Does Jon Boy know the truth?"

Atta nodded. "I confessed to him and only him. The accident was never investigated, so it wasn't anyone's knowledge that the brakes had failed. Drunk driving was stated as the culprit."

"I can't help but wonder how you lived with yourself after that? Please don't think I am being insensitive. I just can't believe—"

"I understand," Atta looked down at her feet. "I failed to cope. I made a rash, foolish decision that night."

Maureen thought about the loving couple who raised her, they were the closest thing to parents she would ever have in her lifetime. "The two of you have been through quite a lot. I mean, I had no idea."

"Of course you wouldn't. It was our responsibility to protect you and Quinn, and to hopefully raise you both with good values."

"I'm forever indebted to you."

"Nonsense."

A little silence was shared again before Maureen spoke. "I'm sitting over here with questions. I want to know why you decided to tell me this? How did you two make it to 57 years together?" Maureen couldn't help but think about her own marriage that just failed after 15 years.

"When the trust is broken, you never fully recover. You just have to decide to let it go or to leave," Atta began to explain. "After Jon vowed to protect me from what I did, I questioned if he was doing that out of manipulation. Did he claim to care that much about me and my freedom, or was he thinking that if he kept my secret, I would be indebted to him and to our marriage — despite his infidelity?"

"So you left?"

"I didn't want to leave my Quinn. She was only six years old at the time, but I knew I wouldn't be any good for her until I figured out my life. I wanted my family intact; I wanted the life we shared together on this farm. But clearly, I was not enough for my husband. He swore otherwise, he begged me not to leave. I left anyway."

Maureen listened raptly. This was the mystery surrounding Atta Palmer, the one subject that was never brought up, never talked about after her hiatus from her family ended.

"My aunt had a cabin in Washington County, just forty-five minutes from here. I stayed there, alone for a while. And then, I met the groundskeeper of the nearby conservation area."

"And?" Maureen already knew the answer coming up. She could see by Atta's expression that the groundkeeper had done more than tidy up the land.

"We had a six-month fling. It was the best sex I've ever had in my life."

"Atta!" Maureen was smirking and feeling awkwardly embarrassed at the same time in front of this eighty-something-year-old woman who was a mother figure to her, always comparable to June Cleaver on the Leave it to Beaver sitcom in the early 1960s.

Atta laughed out loud. "I never intended for it to happen, but how ironic that it did. Perhaps it began as payback to my unfaithful husband, but it gave me perspective. I returned to my family with a better understanding of everything. What I mean is I have never looked back and blamed Jon, or felt guilty for my own actions with a younger man. What was done was done, and we carried on with our life together afterward."

"Does Jon Boy know any of that?"

"I never told him," Atta answered. "You are the only person I've confided in. I see the crossroad you're at. I want you to escape, find a peaceful place, figure out your next move. They say that life doesn't wait for us, but I disagree."

"I don't know what to say," Maureen responded.

"I'm concerned for you. I recognize some of my old self in you. You've lost your purpose."

"I don't see how running away will help me." She had endured enough change in her life in a matter of days and was still struggling to come up for air.

"But what if it does?" Atta reacted.

Chapter 4

As Maureen drove away from the farm, she contemplated her next move. She had no family to go home to. Her son was dead. Her husband was moving on without her. A few miles down the road, she passed her house. She drove on, down Main Street, past the town square. This was the town that built her. It was nothing particularly fancy, but it was growing and flourishing year after year. It was salt of the earth to Maureen. Her roots humbled her. She was born there to her birth parents, but her memories of the first three years of her life were null. Unfortunately, she remembered the foster homes after that. She preferred to hold tight to when her life really began at nine years old. It was Palmer and her parents who saved her. They saw her through those cringeworthy middle years, onto high school, which had been both difficult and spectacular in unparalleled ways. She and Palmer were inseparable then (and still now). They saw each other through everything that mattered then — the grades, the activities, the achievements, the jobs, the crushes, the drama, and the rebellion. Other friends from those years had come and gone from Maureen's life. Some built her up, others tore her down. No one had carved their name into her heart the way Palmer had.

They were best friends. Perhaps even soul mates. She couldn't imagine taking Atta's advice and leaving town for a while. What would she tell Palmer?

Right now, she wanted to track her down and tell her everything. The blanks concerning her mother's getaway months had finally been filled. Yet, Maureen questioned if it would be disrespectful to speak of it. Atta had, after all, bared her soul to help Maureen. What if she had a point? What if space and time somewhere away from all the reminders would be what she needed?

It took longer than it once did to drive that town, end to end, but Maureen did, and then she went home.

As much as Maureen hated to admit it, she felt what Archer said. That house. Their home as a family. It didn't feel the same anymore. It brought her such pain to walk through that front door and not hear or see her son. And to know she would never see him on earth again. She would hold onto the hope to see him again one day in the hereafter. Her faith wasn't strong, it never really had been. The Palmers were Catholic, and they encouraged her to tell them if she ever wanted to be baptized and follow with the seven sacraments to make her a full-fledged member of the Catholic religion to ensure her entrance into heaven one day. Maureen never got into all that. She attended church every weekend with the three of them, and every time Palmer left the pew to receive Holy Communion, she would discreetly give Maureen the finger for being allowed to stay behind and be a nonparticipant. The memory of that still made Maureen giggle.

She sat down on her sofa, pulled her blanket over her lower half, and sent Palmer a text.

It's your fault that I'm not a practicing Catholic. If you hadn't grumbled through every Mass and griped about every sacrament, maybe now I would be closer to God and believing my son will send me some signs that his soul still exists somewhere.

Those words were lighthearted, yet sorrowful, and Palmer's response was exactly what she needed. She flipped her off in the form of a single middle finger emoji.

And then she added a few words, just because.

The Reen I know does not need to go through the proper channels for anything. You ask your boy yourself to send you a damn sign. And he will.

Maureen's reply was simple. It was gratitude.

Thank you.

What have you done with yourself today? Palmer wanted to

keep the conversation going. This time, following her boy's death, was crucial for survival. If Reen reached out, Palmer wanted to be there. Regardless, Palmer would be there.

I went to see your mother.

Our mother. Did she fill you up with fresh-out-of-the-oven baked goods or words of wisdom?

No sweets, but Atta's advice for me is suddenly all I can think about.

I can come over.

You do not have to drop everything to pick me up off the floor.

It's my Catholic faith oozing from my pores. I am a loyal servant to others.

Maureen laughed out loud.

And within several minutes, Palmer walked through her front door without a knock or another word's notice. She plopped down on the sofa and stole some of the blanket for her own lap. "Tell me what's on your mind."

"We have never kept secrets from each other. I have to tell you this, but I also have to ask you to be careful with the truth. I don't want Atta to think that I couldn't wait to blab to you."

"I think she knows us better than that."

"Probably. Just be respectful."

"Reen, I'm an adult."

"Right. What fools we were when we wanted to grow up and make all the big decisions for ourselves, with no one else telling us what to do."

"Is Momma Atta telling you what you should or should not be doing?"

Maureen shook her head. "She thinks I should escape for a while. Just go away and find my peace."

"What? Alone? Reen, you can't run from this. It's going to hurt on the beach or in the mountains, or right here. It's all the same. Why does she think you can outrun the pain?"

"Because she did."

Palmer's eyes widened. "Did she tell you where she was for all those months when I was just a little girl?" A part of Palmer would always feel bitter about that temporary abandonment that was never spoken of.

"She did. Listen, I can't make this shit up, but it's going to seem like I fabricated one hell of a story. Just listen before you react."

Palmer mentally braced herself for something shocking.

First, Maureen explained the cheating scandal, caused by Palmer's father. And Palmer's mother's reaction to it.

"Can I say something? I have to interrupt now," Palmer was adamant. Maureen nodded. She, too, still felt the shock of this, after only knowing the truth for a matter of hours.

"My mother was responsible for her death?"

"Possibly? But, she was driving drunk."

"With no brakes!"

"Right."

"I cannot believe any of this. She just casually told you all that in between rocking her chair on the front porch?"

"I am still as shocked as you."

"So that's why she left? She was running scared?"

"She told me that Jon Boy vowed to protect her, that it would forever be their secret. She also said she felt manipulated to stay in her marriage, as if he would be forgiven for his affair if he manned up and protected her."

"She ran. Okay. I get that. I do. What I don't understand is why she came back and the two of them casually carried on with the rest of their lives as if nothing ever happened."

"We don't know what happened in their marriage, with intimacy at least. We never even saw them kiss, the affection was just nonexistent, and we lived under the same roof. I mean, we probably see and hear more endearment between them now, and they are old."

Palmer didn't disagree. "Where did she go all those months?" She needed to know more about her mother.

"Not very far, believe it or not," Maureen offered. "Remember our eighth-grade field trip to the conservation area in Washington County?"

"Was that the place where we veered off the walking trail, escaped the group, and smoked cigarettes behind some random shed?"

Maureen laughed. "Oh, the memories."

"I could use a cigarette about now."

"You don't smoke."

"This is going to drive me to smoke or drink or do something to erase how I feel knowing the truth."

"I haven't told you the rest of it."

"What was she doing in a conservation area?"

"Apparently there was a cabin nearby that belonged to her aunt. It was vacant and Atta stayed there all those months."

"So, that's it? She found her peace deep in the woods all alone for several months?"

"She wasn't completely alone."

Palmer waited to hear more.

"She met the groundskeeper. I don't know the full story, other than your sweet little momma can be quoted saying she had the best sex of her life with a much younger man."

"Oh my God!"

"Yes. I am still cringing over here."

"So that was her revenge on my dad for cheating first?"

"Seems so."

"So, they repaired their marriage after all that happened between them… and with others?"

"Jon Boy doesn't know that his wife screwed around on him, too."

"Probably best," Palmer noted.

"So now we know."

"I wish I didn't," Palmer's disgust was evident in her tone.

"The bottom line is Atta thinks I should go away for a while to find peace in having to start over with my life."

"So you're going to look to get laid, too?"

Maureen laughed. "I'll let you know if I do."

"I think I'd like to join you on this escape."

"You have a family to take care of."

"I would never leave my kids that way. I am not my mother."

"She made it up to you. She was a wonderful mom."

"I haven't forgotten though. It took me years to stop wondering if she would be gone again when I got home from school. I was only in the first fucking grade. I was so afraid. And clearly, I'm still scarred from the trauma."

Maureen reached for her hand. "Hey, she came back. Feeling like a new woman, too, apparently." They both giggled. "And, you are not going anywhere. You're a good mom to your three." It suddenly pained Maureen to think of Palmer having three children to love when she lost the only one she would ever have.

"Hey," Palmer read the expression on her face. "You can have any one of mine anytime."

"I wouldn't know what to do with girls."

Palmer had three daughters. The oldest was 17 years old and the youngest were 15-year-old twins. Her marriage to Jake had been going strong for two decades. Maureen had always been envious of the balance they created together. With Archer, she had always felt outsmarted and overruled. Unless something pertained to their son, Maureen typically gave in to keep the peace. She never liked being a wife, but she wanted to be a mother every single day of Isaac's life. The question haunted her now, though. Had she failed at being his mother somewhere along the way?

"It's not all that different, Reen. All kids, all kinds, just want to be loved."

"Loving mine wasn't enough for him."

"I am so sorry for what he did."

"Me too." Maureen refused to give in and cry those tears

she felt coming on.

"Please don't listen to Atta this time. Her motherly advice to run at a time, when you need us all the most, sucks."

"I don't know. Archer was right about one thing, it is so hard to be in this house."

"Then move! God knows you could downsize."

"Rash decisions are never good."

"But picking up and leaving is?"

Maureen shrugged. "It's not as permanent."

"Then where? Where do you plan to go?"

"I will tell you when I know. I promise, okay? I'm not going into hiding, but I do see what Atta meant. I could use a change of scenery. I realized that when I came back into this house. I'm losing here, I'm defeated. Every room has a memory that I cannot handle right now."

"I don't like this."

"I don't like my life anymore."

"I know, and I am trying to be supportive instead of selfish. I want you close by. I always have, and I always will."

"I promise not to go far."

"Pack your razor… just in case there's a groundskeeper."

They both threw their heads back laughing.

Chapter 5

Maureen's online research for somewhere secluded but close by, as she promised Palmer, led her to find the Tara Point Inn and Cottages, located high on the hill along the Great River Road in Grafton, Illinois. She reserved a one-bedroom cottage for a month… and decided she would take it from there.

Aside from packing her clothes and necessities into suitcases, she also put her favorite blanket, the Keurig for her daily coffee, and at the last minute she put her boy's cell phone inside her handbag. She still had not opened his bedroom door. She was not ready for that, but his phone had been in her bedroom since the night Archer left and she had stopped him from taking it. She thought of Archer now, but only for a moment. Not a single text or phone call had been exchanged between the two of them. It was almost as if he was dead, too. Only there was no sadness in her soul for her now estranged husband.

Maureen closed up the house, window blinds and all. It felt strange leaving there, as she once believed it would be her forever home. After starting her car in the garage, she backed out. With the car engine running idle on the driveway, she attempted to close her side of the garage, but the door would not budge. She blamed the battery, got out of the car, and walked into the garage to close the door. She exited through the side door of the house, and then locked it. As she turned around to walk toward her car on the driveway, something caught her eye across the street. Adam and Jamie were their neighbors for as long as they lived in that subdivision. They had two children, a boy and a girl, and always seemed like the all-American family. They had been incredibly supportive the last several days, Maureen noted, but then she realized that since Archer left, she had not seen or heard from them, Jamie especially was the one who had been coming in and out of their house most, as if it had a revolving door.

That's who she saw now. Across the street, Jamie was getting out of her car on the driveway, and someone else was in the passenger seat. It wasn't Adam. That much, Maureen could see for sure. She stared. Jamie waved awkwardly. Maureen wasn't so sure what got into her, but she started walking down her driveway, past her vehicle with the engine running, and across the street toward Jamie.

"Hey, got a minute?" Maureen called out.

"Actually, I was just about to—" Before Jamie could explain, Maureen was standing close enough to get a better look at who was inside her car. Her initial instincts were proven right. It was Archer.

There had been so much shock and upset in her life lately that what she was seeing did not instantly register in her mind. Maureen just stood there, staring. Jamie wore a look of sheer shame. And Archer looked screwed. It was the expression on his face that snapped Maureen out of the fog she was submerged in. Her husband looked guilty.

"Archer?" Maureen glanced from him to her always kind and supportive neighbor, Jamie. "I thought Adam was in there," she addressed Jamie, to purposely put her on the spot. *Where is your own husband and why are you with mine?*

"Adam and I are separated."

"How did I not know this?" Maureen again glanced from Jamie to Archer. He stayed silent, which was a rarity in itself. She wanted to ask where his vehicle was, why he was stowed away in their neighbor's car, but the answer was obvious. They were hiding from her.

"We still do things together for the kids… and we were, of course, united for Isaac's funeral."

Those two words strung together… *Isaac's funeral*… momentarily stabbed at Maureen's chest. *Would the reality of her son being dead ever feel less heavy?*

"I don't understand," Maureen stated. "I would have never guessed the two of you were having problems." Under normal circumstances, she would have said she was sorry to hear that, but Archer's presence was blatantly clear right now and it trumped everything else. "What is going on between the two of you?"

Finally, Archer stepped out of the car. The sunlight on his dark hair highlighted the sporadic gray. At fifty, he still wanted to pull off being a couple decades younger, but Father Time wasn't stalling.

"Are you sleeping with her?" Maureen called him out.

"We're separated, Reen," his tone reeked of arrogance. The coward she previously witnessed slinking on the passenger seat of another woman's car was suddenly gone. "Who I sleep with is no concern of yours."

"We are still married."

"There's nothing left between us," he said to her, and those words stung again. *Nothing was left. Their son was gone. Nothing bonded them anymore.*

"How long has this been going on?"

She noticed Jamie's long dark hair was tied up in a messy bun, which somehow drew more attention to her pointed nose. This neighbor, this person Maureen considered to be a friend, looked down at the concrete, while Archer stepped closer to her.

Maureen watched her look up at him and when he turned to her, Maureen suddenly felt as if she was invisible. The look she watched them exchange nearly knocked the wind out of her. Whether it was love or lust or something else, they looked happy together. And the only thing that Maureen could feel at that moment was nothing. It was a complete shock to her that Archer was having an affair with the neighbor, a friend of theirs, but she couldn't have cared less. She wasn't hurt, or jealous, or even livid. She was simply done. Maureen turned on her heels as she threw her hands up in the air. "Do what you want with your life. Neither one of you are worth the energy to me anymore."

Maureen never looked back. Later, as she made the one-hour drive to Great River Road, she would think about how effortless leaving her home ended up feeling, after knowing that there truly was nothing left for her there.

Chapter 6

The cottage that Maureen chose was on the riverfront, situated on eighty acres of land with additional winding river frontage to explore. Maureen could already see herself taking long hikes to clear her mind and to keep active. Inside, the cottage was cozy and cute. It had a small kitchen, a living area with a fireplace, and down the hallway was one bedroom and one bathroom. She laughed when she saw the old-time clawfoot bathtub in the middle of the bathroom. There was also a corner, stand-alone shower with a glass door. Maureen told herself that she would have everything she needed here. At least for a little while.

She stopped in town at a grocery store along the way and now had plenty of food for a few days, but she wasn't interested in cooking or eating anything. She didn't feel like unpacking either. That was the thing about grief. It came in waves and when it hit her, she was completely at a loss. She hurt in places that were difficult to pinpoint because the pain in her heart overflowed into every crevice that existed inside her body. Maureen made her way into the back bedroom. Her suitcases stood upright on the floor by the bed. She sunk down on that bed, and the tears came as she gave in to the hopelessness she felt. Her son was gone. Her life was different now and would always be. The rest of the world just kept on, but her entire world had come to a complete halt, as if she was stuck in some sort of metaphorical mud, and not able to move. Thoughts of Isaac consumed her as she curled her body on the bed, sobbing, and eventually whimpering herself to sleep.

The sunrise, through the open window blinds in the bedroom, woke her. She was disoriented at first. Then she remembered where she was, and she immediately wondered if she had even locked the door to the cottage last night. She was so overcome with emotion that she had been unable to think clearly. *Welcome to grief,* she thought, and forced her body off the bed.

After a shower, a cup of coffee and two scrambled eggs, Maureen pulled on a pair of jeans and a hoodie. She stepped outside to see what the grounds could offer her. Peace of mind was top on her list today.

The grounds —the colorful leaves on the trees, the landscape, and the water— took her breath away. Maureen had no idea how far she had walked, but she reminded herself that she still needed to make her way back. Some of the boundless energy that she felt out there had to be reserved for her return trip. As she was going to turn around, she noticed the tree line gave way to a view of houses at the foot of the hill. When she stepped closer and peered through the brush, she saw movement on the loading dock near the river.

There was a child. He appeared to be alone. He was wearing a red baseball cap. Maureen tried not to think about Isaac at that age, five or six, and his love of all things baseball. One wall in his bedroom had enough pegs to hang fifteen caps. That was then, his bedroom had changed since. And now it sat empty and untouched, as her boy would forever be fourteen. She started to walk the downhill path to that small dock. Part of her was curious what he was doing out there alone, and perhaps the mother in her wanted to be sure he was safe near the water.

She watched him skip rocks. He looked like he'd done that before, throwing stones into the lake in a way that made them jump across the surface of the water. By the time she got closer, he didn't seem as focused on the rocks. He was spinning around, acting silly like a child does, and that's when he lost his balance. His cap flew off, he tried to catch it, but it went airborne off the dock and into the river. He got too close to the edge, suddenly lying flat on his belly, reaching his arm out as far as he could, but the cap was already moving away from his grasp. Maureen picked up her pace and ran onto the dock. The little boy was startled by her at first, but he immediately asked her to help him.

"You lost your cap when it fell in the water?" Maureen was cautious not to scare him further.

"Please help me get it! It's from my mom. It's special."

The word, *mom,* coming from a little boy instantly affected Maureen and sent her into help mode. She stepped out of her shoes, she pulled her hoodie over her head. Luckily, she wore a full-coverage sports bra underneath. The water would be cold, she knew that, but she was going in anyway. The current had yet to take the red cap, bobbing out there on the surface of the water. She bent down to the child. "You stay here, okay? Do not leave this dock. I will go into that water and bring your cap back." He nodded. She turned and bravely jumped into the river. When her head surfaced, she only had about twenty feet to swim to reach the cap. The cold water was an annoyance, not a danger. It was only October, so the air temperature had not yet reached freezing.

Maureen gripped the cap firmly in one hand and swam back to the dock. The little boy was waiting for her at the edge. He was on his belly again and he reached his tiny hand out to her. Maureen was treading water beneath him. "Here, take your cap. I will pull myself up. I don't want to be too much weight for you, or we will both end up swimming."

He giggled. She felt a pang in her heart.

After two attempts to pull her body weight up, Maureen was struggling. There was just too much height between the dock and the water. Her arm muscles could not handle pulling up her entire bodyweight. And now she was getting cold, submerged in the water.

She thought of asking the boy if he was out there by himself, did he live nearby, could he go get someone to help? She also considered swimming to a lower edge, even if it was grass. She could latch on. But, before she did anything, the boy above her called out to someone.

"Dad! Dad! I'm over here. Help this lady in the water. She saved my favorite ballcap!"

A second later, Maureen was looking up at a man beside the boy. He was an adult version of the child. Brown hair, brown eyes, a kind face — a handsome face. "Grab ahold of my hand, I will pull you up."

Maureen reached. She felt this man's grip on her. It was strong and reassuring. In a matter of seconds, he had her. One arm, both arms, her torso, her waist. He just kept getting a better grip on her, the higher he lifted her. She was on the dock now, and she quickly got to her feet. "You okay?" he asked, and she thought about this scene. What just happened. What she might look like standing there drenched in her socks, her jeans, and her bra. *Shit.* She glanced down at the dock to search for her hoodie, but she was distracted when she realized she had not answered his question. "Yes, I'm okay. We saved the cap." She looked down at the boy, wide-eyed beside his father. He smiled.

"You saved the cap. You jumped in the water for it."

She smiled back.

His father spoke again.

"I'm Andy, and this is my son, Joey."

"I'm Maureen. Most call me Reen."

"I think Reen is a fun name," Joey reacted.

"Yeah?" Maureen held in a giggle. "I guess it is kind of fun. Thank you."

A moment of awkward smiles between them prompted Maureen to spring into action to get dressed. "I need to find my shirt."

"I saw it over there," Andy spoke, and Joey ran to retrieve it for her. She hurried to pull it over her head, to cover her bare chest. Well, it wasn't bare, but she was wearing minimal clothing on the top half of her body in front of strangers. It did feel wonderful to be wearing something dry on her otherwise soaking wet body.

"Thank you," Maureen focused on Joey as she crossed her arms over her chest. He was standing there holding his ballcap. It was too wet to wear — but he clearly gripped it for dear life as he was so relieved it was not lost to him forever.

"No," Joey spoke up, "thank you for helping me. My mom gave me this cap."

"Well I'm sure your mom will be very happy that you still have your favorite ballcap."

"I don't know if I am going to be able to tell her." His shoulders slumped, and Maureen fleetingly glanced at Andy. She wasn't sure if she overstepped, and if she did, she wished she could take it back. The last thing she wanted to hear was another sad story of life.

"Joey's mom needed to take a little break. She's on a getaway to hit the reset button," Andy vaguely explained, and

Maureen assumed those were all words he had already told his son.

"I understand a reset," she admitted.

"Do you live here? Or, are you on a trip, like my mom?"

"I am on a trip. I am staying in one of those cottages on the other side of the hill." She pointed and Joey looked far in the distance as if he would be able to see it from where they stood on the riverbank.

"What color is it?" the little boy was curious.

"Pale yellow."

"Oh," Joey was intrigued with the extra adjective to describe the color yellow. "My house is firetruck red."

She smiled, and so did his dad.

"Joey, why don't you run ahead, and I will meet you at home in two minutes?" Andy suggested, and Maureen wished he hadn't. She really did not want to get involved or hear anything else that would make her heart hurt.

"But I like her, dad. She's pretty, and she saved my cap."

Maureen smiled. "Well I don't feel so pretty dripping wet from head to toe, but thank you. You go on home, I have to do the same."

Joey stepped toward her. There wasn't an ounce of bashfulness in his body. He showed complete confidence as he wrapped his arms around her upper legs. "Bye Reen."

She inhaled.

When he ran off, Maureen was still trying to regulate her breathing. Joey reminded her of Isaac. Or perhaps she just wanted that to feel true.

"You okay?" That was the second time this man, this stranger, sensed something was wrong.

Maureen nodded. "I just need to reset. I like that word, that idea, by the way."

He smiled, but it quickly faded as he spoke again. "My wife left us. I don't know if she's coming back... for Joey."

"I'm so sorry." What else could she say? "I do hope she just needs to sort some things out." There. That was kind, but not intrusive.

"I really appreciate what you did for Joey. It was dangerous, and you shouldn't have, but thank you. As you know, that cap is sentimental."

Maureen paused before she said what she wanted to say.

"It was worth it. I do owe you for fishing me out of the water though."

He laughed. "My pleasure."

"I should go." She stepped back and slipped into her shoes without untying the laces.

"Can I drive you? Those cottages are quite a hike from here."

"Thank you, but I need the exercise."

She saw him look at her. She got the feeling he was going to compliment her, and suddenly she was embarrassed that he saw her partially unclothed on top. She cringed at the afterthought of her boobs likely popping out of that sports bra as he lifted her from the water. There was no need to revisit that moment, she just needed to go now.

"Okay," he agreed to let her walk back. "Be safe. And, Reen... I hope you find that reset button sooner than later."

She smiled. She liked how that sounded. "Me too, Andy."

Chapter 7

The hike back to her cottage wasn't nearly as pleasant. Maureen was wet, cold, and tired by the time she returned. She stripped down, showered, and could not wait to blow dry her hair. She thought again of Joey and his dad. She was grateful the ballcap was saved, and relieved she was able to help. Everyone needed something to hold onto when their lives were turned upside-down. For her, however, she wasn't so sure what was left.

There were three messages from Palmer on her phone when she finally checked it. It had been on the kitchen counter charging since she left for her hike. She hadn't bothered to take it with her earlier, and after jumping in the river, she was glad of that.

The messages from Palmer were basically summed up as she wanted to know if she was settling in, how safe she felt there, and then she added that if she didn't respond to her messages, she was going to drive up to the Great River Road herself.

Maureen smiled. And then instead of texting, she called her. Palmer answered on the second ring.

"Reener… how are you?"

Maureen shrugged. "Is 'better than ever' too much of an embellishment?"

This time Palmer grinned on the opposite end of the phone. "You must have met the groundskeeper already," she quipped, and Maureen caught herself thinking of Andy… and his little boy, Joey.

"We have to stop making fun of that," Maureen said with laughter in her tone.

"I don't think I can deal with it if I don't find some humor there."

"That was a long time ago. Let's give Atta some slack."

"Tell me about you and how it's going there all alone."

"It's not like I'm truly isolated here. There are other people out and about."

"Just be safe, Reen. We don't need any more craziness in our lives." It was heartwarming to Maureen knowing that they were bonded so closely that when something happened to one of them, it happened to the other just the same.

"Actually, do you want to hear something a tad crazy that already happened here?"

"Sure, as long as you tell me that you're keeping your doors locked."

"That might defeat the purpose when I have all my windows open."

Palmer laughed.

"So I set out for a long hike this morning. I ended up near a neighborhood, and I left the trail when I saw a little boy on the riverbank. He was playing, skipping rocks, all that, and then he lost his red ballcap."

"In the water?"

"Yes, and he was so close to the water, trying to reach for it."

"Oh my God, he fell in, and you went in after him?" Palmer's assumption wasn't that far off.

"Just the cap. I went in for the cap. He said it was special to him, so I jumped in and got it."

"That could have gone all sorts of wrong," Palmer stated as fact. "How cold was that water?"

"Chilly. And yes, I know." Maureen paused. "I live my life differently now. It really doesn't matter if I take risks."

"It does matter, Reen." Palmer didn't have to tell her that she wouldn't survive a single day of her life without her lifelong friend. "So you saved the cap and then what? Did that child have any supervision out there near the water?"

"I had the worst time pulling myself out of the water after I swam for the cap. There was too much height between the water I was treading in and the dock above. Luckily, Joey's dad was nearby."

"Joey's dad pulled you out of the water?"

"He did. His name is Andy. But what an awkward introduction that was with me drenched and shirtless."

Palmer laughed out loud. "Was he good looking?"

"Yes. That's what made it so embarrassing."

"Did he think you were ridiculous for risking your life for a cap? I'm sure the kid has a ton… just like Isaac used to."

Maureen didn't mind Palmer bringing up the memory, but she knew so many others would forever tiptoe around ever mentioning her son again. If they were worried about upsetting her, making her sad, that was pointless. She would always be sad, but more than anything she wanted to keep his memory alive remembering him and talking about him. For the love of God, say his name.

"I thought of Isaac, too… and the wall in his bedroom with all the hanging caps that multiplied every time we went shopping anywhere. Running an errand meant he would sucker me into buying him a new ballcap." Maureen smiled at the memory, as Palmer stayed silent and allowed her to relive it. "And, no, his dad was very happy the cap was saved. It was sentimental because Joey's mom gave it to him… and apparently she recently took off."

"For good, or Atta style?"

They both laughed.

"Hopefully she will be back. Andy explained it as she needed a reset."

"That's an interesting way to put it."

"I said the same," Maureen agreed. "I wish I could find the reset button myself. But the thing is, what am I resetting? I don't have any part of my life that I could bring back and be better at."

"What if Archer comes back and wants to save your marriage?"

Maureen scoffed a little. "Archer is screwing our neighbor. Remember Jamie? A so-called friend?"

"How do you know this, and what happened to her husband?"

"I was the last to know they are separated and have been for a while," Maureen explained what she knew for sure. "I saw the two of them across the street. I was backing out of my driveway. She pulled up to her house and Archer was hiding in the passenger seat. I guess they thought it would hurt me if their secret got out when I saw his vehicle parked on her driveway."

"Did you confront him?"

"I did. He made a point to tell me that we are separated, so whoever he sleeps with is none of my business."

"Asshole."

"I don't want to talk about Archer anymore."

"I'm sorry that everything has fallen apart, Reen." Palmer didn't know what else to say.

"I'm beyond sorry that my son is gone," Maureen caught her breath, "but my marriage has been over for a long time. We were broken before Isaac did what he did."

"I know that. And I know you both chose to stay together because of him, but that was not healthy for any of you."

"Are you implying that my son was unhappy because his parents didn't love each other?"

"I don't know," Palmer answered honestly. "Like you, I cannot explain what could have been that bad in his mind, bad enough to end his life."

"I brought his phone with me here," Maureen told her.

"Do you think there's a clue somewhere in there?"

"If so, it won't change the fact that he's gone."

"You're afraid," Palmer chose her words cautiously.

Maureen was silent for a moment.

"Yes… a part of me doesn't even want to know. That same part of me thinks what if it was something trivial that only teenagers think is godawful. What if I could have fixed it, if I had known."

"Reen. Listen to me. Isaac didn't give you a chance to fix anything. It's not your fault. What he did was not something you could have stopped. Not if he wanted to do it that badly."

"I hear those words, but I can't process them. Not yet."

"I wish you weren't an hour away," Palmer said, wanting to run to her.

"I like it here."

"You just want to see that hottie at the riverbank again."

Maureen laughed. Honestly, though, she had been thinking more about Joey. His tender heart had been so consumed with losing a ballcap, which to him was symbolic of his mother who had left him. For Maureen, that short time with him, felt like a little bit of heaven.

Chapter 8

Maureen returned from a quick trip to the grocery store. She wanted to make a pot of homemade chicken soup. Her appetite still wasn't the best, but soup appealed to her today. She also picked up two bottles of white wine. Sometimes at night, she needed something to calm her mind before bed.

She parked her car outside of the cottage and carried everything in one trip. When she reached the porch, she stopped. On the top step was a vase of six long-stemmed roses, one half were orange, and the other half were peach. There was a card attached. She set down everything she was carrying on the bottom step, climbed to the top step, and sat beside the vase. She opened the small envelope to read the message on the card.

The handwriting was clearly a beginner, and she knew right away who it was.

Dear Reen,

Thank you for saving my ballcap in the water. These flowers are for you. My dad said the colors mean something special. Peach is because I am thankful for what you did. Orange is because you made me happy.

Joey

Maureen had tears in her eyes when she held the card against her chest, over her heart. That boy. She was sorry she missed his visit to her cottage, but she hoped she would see him again very soon.

After she went inside to unpack those few groceries, Maureen knew that making soup could wait. Instead of hiking this time, she drove to the neighborhood that sat below the hillside near the riverbank.

She looked for a firetruck red house.

When she walked up to the front door, which was painted charcoal gray, she wondered if this would seem weird, coming there. But there was no other way for her to thank Joey for the flowers — and she wanted him to know that she was touched.

She pressed her finger to the doorbell once, and she instantly heard running feet. It had been a long time since she heard Isaac race through the house, feet pounding on the wood flooring. The teenage years had made those trips from room to room inside the house a little more subtle. Depending on his mood, those size ten and a half feet were dragging sometimes. *Teenagers.*

The door flew open, and Joey was standing there with a wide smile. "We saw you on our ring doorbell camera!" Slightly embarrassed, Maureen laughed. It was a good thing she had not lost her courage and turned around to leave. She wouldn't have. She really wanted to thank Joey.

"I'll bet you know why I'm here," Maureen stated, and he repeatedly nodded his head of thick brown hair.

"The flowers are beautiful, and thank you for the special note attached, too."

"My dad helped me with the colors, I mean I wanted to know what they meant in words."

Maureen could not stop smiling. Her heart hadn't felt this full in a very long time. "I had no idea what those particular colors meant."

"We googled that."

Maureen laughed out loud.

"It was very special." She wanted those flowers to live forever. She knew all too well, though, how nothing lasted forever.

"You can come inside my house," Joey stepped back.

"I shouldn't. I'm sure you and your dad are busy today."

Joey spun his body around. "My dad is here, right behind me, standing against the wall listening to us talk."

Now, it was Andy who felt awkward. He stepped forward, into plain sight, giving that move his best nonchalant effort.

Maureen exhaled.

"Hello, Andy. Thank you for helping Joey with the flowers. As I told him, they are beautiful."

"My dad bought them, since I don't have any money for expensive things."

Andy tousled his son's hair and chuckled.

"You can come in, if you'd like," Andy invited her.

How could she say no?

"Maybe for a few minutes."

The space inside the house wasn't immense like Maureen was used to back home, but everything from the furniture to the appliances was new and modern. It was tidy, considering two males were living there alone.

While they were walking through the kitchen and living area, Andy had to take a phone call. When he stepped away, Joey filled in the blanks. "My dad owns a roofing company. He started at the bottom when he was a teenager. Well, not the bottom, he was on the roof." The more Joey talked, the more she adored him. He took her hand and led her out the patio door. There was a swimming pool, covered for the fall and winter seasons, and there was also a small basketball court with just one hoop.

"Come watch me shoot."

Maureen stepped outside with him, and suddenly Andy followed.

The two of them stood at the perimeter of the court watching. Only a few minutes passed before the neighbor boy ran over to Joey and the two of them started playing together. But first, Joey called out to her.

"This is my friend, Brandon. He lives next door. And this is Maureen, people call her Reen. She's the one who saved my ballcap in the river."

Maureen waved and laughed to herself as Andy spoke. "You're forever going to be labeled as the rockstar who saved the ballcap."

"Absolutely. I'm a hero," Maureen embellished.

"To him, you are."

She made direct eye contact with him. Andy wasn't a tall man, not like Archer at 6'3." If she had to guess, he was right at six-foot, because she was 5'7" and she didn't have to look up much to see his brown eyes.

He broke the stares between them.

"Would you like to go sit on the patio? We will still be able to see them playing. I could get you a drink or something?"

She agreed. "I'll have whatever's convenient for you."

"It's almost noon. White wine, okay?"

She laughed because, at first, she thought he was joking.

"I just bought two bottles today at the grocery store."

"Then we have something in common. Good taste in wine. I'll be right back. Go ahead and sit wherever you'd like."

Maureen found a spot under the covered patio. She sat down where she had a good view of Joey and his friend.

A few minutes later, Andy joined her with a plate of crackers and cheese, two glasses, and a bottle of wine. "Thought we better have something to soak up the alcohol."

She laughed. She was doing a lot of that when she was around Joey and his dad.

Maureen grabbed a chunk of brick cheese while Andy poured them both a glass of wine. "So, Joey mentioned that you own a roofing company."

"I do. It's a business that just sort of found me in my

teenage years, and I never left."

"It's important to love what you do." This was the first time in over a week that Maureen actually thought of her job and missed feeling productive. She watched Andy stack two pieces of cheese on a cracker, one white and one yellow, and then he ate it. He washed that down with a swallow of wine before he spoke again.

"You know that I have Joey... and my wife left us. You also know that I run my own business. Let's even the score. Tell me about Reen." She was beautiful, Andy could not deny that. When he saw her on the ring doorbell camera on his phone, he looked twice. Her long blonde hair had been soaking wet the first time he met her. This time, those locks were wavy and bouncy, down to her shoulders.

Maureen took a sip of her wine. She was already halfway through drinking one glass and was suddenly grateful for the liquid courage. "My job or my personal life?"

"Whatever you would like to share," Andy encouraged her.

"I was an orphan at three years old," she started from the beginning, and surprised herself with that admission. She took another swig of wine. "My parents were too young to raise me, they tried, but eventually split, and then abandoned me. I spent several years in foster homes, never the same one for very long.

Then, in the fourth grade, I was nine years old when I met my forever family."

"You finally found the right foster home?" Andy's heart went out to her.

"No. I found my best friend, Palmer. She took me home and I never left. Her parents raised me as their own. They are in their eighties now, but still going strong."

"And your friendship with Palmer?"

"She's like the air I breathe. I need her to survive. In the most non-lesbian way, she and I are bonded for life."

Andy laughed a little.

"Are either of you married?"

"Palmer and Jake are the perfect couple, married for a couple decades with three great-looking kids. I married Archer fifteen years ago, and just last week, we separated, and we will be divorced sooner than later. There's no room in our marriage for his lover."

"I'm sorry," Andy frowned. "Clearly the guy has no idea what he had." Maybe the alcohol was giving him courage too.

She blushed. Maybe it was the wine. Either way, there was definite heat on her cheeks. "We grew apart. I never cheated on him, and I don't know if he has done this before or not. Truth is, I don't even care."

"Reen, it still hurts, no matter what you tell yourself."

His words were true.

"Some people are good at being in love. We weren't," Maureen began to explain. "The romantic part — sex all the time, the laughs, the long conversations, having fun doing anything at all, and the separation anxiety when you're apart — eventually fades. And sometimes that's when the love goes away, too. When the excitement is gone, the stress of life sets in. The butterflies disappear, the sex becomes a chore, the tears, the sadness, the arguments, the letdowns — it all just takes over. We saw the best in each other, but eventually brought out the worst."

"I think you just described my marriage… and how it also fell apart," Andy admitted. "We grew apart, but that was no excuse for her to leave her son."

"I completely agree," Maureen told him.

"Did the two of you have any children?" It was expected. It was one of the questions that everyone just asked, and the answer was a simple yes or no. But sometimes it wasn't that easy.

Maureen tipped back the last of the wine in her glass. Andy put his hand on the bottle, and she lifted her glass for him to pour her some more. "I swear I'm not a drunk, but I could use one more glass to get through this conversation."

Andy looked concerned but obliged.

"Our son, Isaac." She was careful not to say we *have* a son, or even, we *had* a son. But then she realized she needed to just explain that he was gone. "He was fourteen. He will forever be fourteen to all who knew him. He died. Just last week, he took his own life."

Andy sat up straighter, and immediately reached for her hand on the table. He never said a word, but she could see the compassion in his eyes, and she allowed herself to be comforted by his touch.

"We don't know why; we may never know. That's why I'm here. I need a reset."

He was touched because she used his word. "You're not alone, Reen. You said so yourself, Palmer is your lifeline, and those parents the two of you share sound like they are absolutely wonderful human beings."

A few tears escaped down her cheeks. "I know. I guess I want to be alone to figure out my life. I'm done with the loss. I mean, how much can be taken away from one person?" Her tone changed. "How can I be expected to just carry on every damn time? Especially this. I can survive not having birth parents, I can handle getting a divorce, but I cannot even begin to understand why my son is gone." She cried. Full blown tears. She put her head down on the table and sobbed. This time, though, she wasn't alone. Her sorrow didn't have to be something that she drowned in and then finally forced herself up for air after pure exhaustion. This time, someone else was there for her. Andy dropped to his knees on the stamped concrete beside her chair. He wrapped his arms around her. She lifted her head and fell against his chest. He was strong and comforting, and she was borderline intoxicated and sad and showing him her overwhelming grief.

Finally, when she felt spent, she pulled back from his embrace. "I'm sorry. It comes in waves. I'm sure a bit too much alcohol exposed my vulnerability in spades."

"Why are you apologizing or looking for an excuse? Reen, you have to feel your way through this. I cannot imagine your pain, but I know how important it is to face what hurts us."

They were suddenly startled by Joey standing on the patio near their table. His friend was in the background, as if he was too timid to get close. "Dad? Reen? What's wrong?" The sight had to have looked odd. Andy was on his knees beside her chair and she was crying.

"Reen is sad about something."

"Can we help?" Joey asked her.

"You have helped by being my friend," Reen told him as she wiped the tears off her face with her fingers.

"Okay," he said. "I was going to ask if I could go over to Brandon's house and play, but I am now wondering if I should stay and help with Reen."

Andy looked at Reen and then back at Joey. "I think it's

okay if you go play."

Joey stepped closer to the table. "I don't want you to be sad, and I hope whatever hurts your heart will get better."

"Me too, Joey. Thank you."

When Joey ran off to join his friend, Andy stood, and so did Maureen. He was going to give her some space and sit back down, but she began collecting the things on the table. "I can help you carry this inside. I should probably go back to the cottage soon."

"You don't have to... clean up... or leave."

She gathered the wine glasses anyway, and he helped. They both walked into the house together. In the kitchen, the wine glasses were in the sink and the tray of crackers and cheese was on the counter when Reen turned around and Andy was right in front of her. "Excuse me," he said, softly.

"No, I'm in your way."

"You're not," he reacted. Again, she noticed he wasn't that much taller than her, which made looking at his eyes effortless. She exhaled. "There's still so much I want to know about you. I mean, you know I'm all about having a solid roof. It's only fair that I know what you do for a living."

She laughed a little, and again felt grateful to him for that feeling. "I am a writer. Palmer and I run a local newspaper business in Highland. We were both journalism majors in college."

"That's interesting," Andy grinned.

"It's a lot of work sometimes, grueling hours to meet deadlines, but it has its rewards. A local newspaper gives back to the community, and we both have always shared that goal."

"So you've taken a break from the office for a while too?"

She nodded. "I do feel guilty about that, leaving it all to Palmer."

"I'm sure she understands."

"Right. No one gets me like she does, and that goes both ways for her and I."

"I know she's not that far away, but I just want you to know that I am here, at the bottom of the hill, if you ever need to talk. My shoulder is pretty sturdy too."

His broad shoulders were solid and muscular and sexy. Maureen lost herself in looking at him for a moment. She reached for him and pressed her palms to his chest. "I see that. I feel that."

He took a minute to regroup. Her hands on him were sending signals to the lower parts of his body. She exhaled. And neither one of them were sure which one moved in closer first. It was just one of those times that everything happened too quickly to process how or why. Their lips met. Their mouths opened. Their tongues collided.

Maureen could taste the wine. Hers. Or his. She was lost in him, carried away with what they were doing. The kissing intensified. The touching started. Her lower back was against the counter. His body was pressed against hers.

And then he backed away.

"Joey. He could be home at any moment. I don't want him to see us like this. It would be hard to explain."

"Right, given the fact that you are still married to his mom. I'm married, too, for that matter, so don't think I'm being judgmental."

"I'm sorry if I took this too far. I just wanted to… I still want to… be with you." Andy's words struck her. She felt it, too, though. She wanted him. No explanations. No thinking. Just sex with this man that she just met but somehow felt connected to.

"Can you find out when Joey is coming home?"

Andy's eyes widened. He took his cell phone out of his pocket. He sent a text to Brandon's mom. The reply came back instantly. "I said that I'm dealing with a work issue, and I need thirty minutes."

"I need you," she said to him. "I don't know want to think. I just want to feel."

Andy took her hand and led her down the hallway of his home. "This is the spare bedroom," he told her, and she knew why he clarified which bed he was taking her to.

ALMOST

He closed the door behind them, and the two of them met in the middle of the room with intensity and passion. They kissed long and hard. They started to tear off each other's clothes. This was not going to be getting to know each other's bodies kind of sex. This was going to be explosive and passionate. They both knew that. And besides, they only had so much time.

Chapter 9

It was the wine. That's how Maureen justified what she did with Andy Perry. She learned his last name when they were lying in the afterglow of sex.

"Ryan," she had said aloud, naked in his arms.

"Should I be aware of a man named Ryan in your life?" he partially teased her.

"It's my last name. I don't think I ever told you that."

With a laugh, he responded, "Perry."

"Nice to meet you, Andy Perry."

"Likewise, Reen Ryan," he kissed her full on the mouth.

"You're reigniting the fire," she warned him, "and we don't have enough time."

Maureen now got lost in that memory. His hands on her, his mouth on her. She never had better sex in her life. She also hadn't gotten naked with a man on a first date. Ever. And this had not even been a date! Maureen again blamed the wine.

She still had not unpacked the two suitcases that were on the floor in her bedroom. She was living out of them as if she were staying at a hotel. Maureen wondered if that mirrored how she really felt about being there. Did it feel like home? Of course it didn't. Home, to her, would always been Isaac. And now he was gone forever. She thought of Jon Boy and Atta. They were not getting any younger, they had given her so much all her life. She loved them like parents she never had. And then there was Palmer. Her soul sister. But, Jon Boy and Atta had each other, as Palmer had a family of her own. It was a different kind of feeling when you knew that you had people in your life who cared about you, but at the end of the day you went home alone. Even Andy and Joey had each other. She walked out of the single bedroom at the cottage, leaving the suitcases untouched.

A post-it note was left on the counter, where she walked in the kitchen to pour herself a cup of coffee. She didn't want to lose it, but she also hadn't logged his number into her phone yet. Andy had written it down after she told him she left her phone at the cottage. It wasn't awkward with Andy, but they may have both been wondering if what they did ended there. Maureen believed so. All Andy said, when he handed her his number, was he had hoped she would reach out. He never asked for hers, which had taken the pressure off her as she was preparing to leave his house following their unexpected romp. Was unexpected even the right word? For Maureen, it was out of character. She was trying to ignore the fact that even though she didn't even know Andy Perry, the intimacy they shared felt familiar. She shook off that feeling. The last thing she needed right now was to get involved with a married man whose wife would likely return home to pick up where she left off with her family. That woman had to be out of her mind abandoning a boy like Joey. Surely, she would come back, just as Atta returned to Palmer all those years ago.

Maureen had gone to Great River Road as an escape, and ultimately to find peace. She reminded herself of that just as her phone on the counter rang. It was Palmer.

"Hey there," Maureen answered the call.

"Did I catch you on a hike?" Palmer was aware of how far Maureen ventured away from the cottage she was staying in, and she wanted to verify her whereabouts before she got into what was going on.

"No. I'm at the cottage." Because Maureen and Palmer had known each other for ages, it was never difficult to read their body language or the mere tone in their voice. Maureen instantly knew something was wrong. "Tell me what's going on."

"It's dad. The ambulance just took him from the farm. He had a heart attack in the combine. It was a while... it may have been too long before anyone realized he was in distress."

Jon Boy. That man was of course like a father to Maureen, too. She knew a day like this could come, but not now. Not after she just buried her son. *Was the universe, or God, or whoever was calling the shots, really that cruel?*

"I am leaving now. Give me an hour, or less, depending on traffic."

"Reen. Be careful. Meet us at St. Joe's." By saying *us*, Maureen knew she meant Atta, and she feared for her and the panic she was feeling.

"Keep Atta calm," was all Maureen said before she ended the call and rushed into the back bedroom. How ironic that she had not unpacked. She lifted both suitcases, one with each hand, and scurried out the door to her car, which was parked on the rocked driveway.

She slammed the trunk lid after putting both suitcases inside in a hurry. Once she was behind the wheel, she started the engine, and then shifted the gear into reverse as she spoke out loud. "I don't pray. You know that." She was speaking to God.

"I've never read a single page in your Bible. I go about things my own way. You know what happened the last time I begged you to help me. Don't take Jon Boy from me too."

Chapter 10

Fifty minutes later, she was driving on Troxler Avenue, turning into the parking lot of St. Joseph's Hospital in Highland. She found an open spot close enough to the emergency room, and she sprinted through the lot, up onto the sidewalk, and through the automatic doors of the entrance.

The moment she looked to her left, into the waiting area, she saw both Palmer and Atta, seated side by side on two chairs against the wall. The urgency that she felt to get there suddenly began to diminish. The look on their faces crushed her. Atta spoke first the moment Maureen made her way over to them.

"Sit down by us, Reen."

"I've been sitting for the last hour. Please, just tell me how Jon Boy is doing."

Palmer looked down, and Maureen's heart sank. She was going to let Atta tell her that her father, *their father*, was gone.

Maureen bent to her knees on the floor directly in front of Atta. She placed her hands on hers. Those once hardworking hands, now aged with wrinkled lines and sunspots. Maureen remembered a time when those hands were plumper and softer, instead of frail and bony. "I typically sit on the front porch and watch him when he's in the field," Atta began to explain. "I was doing something else inside the house. I didn't know that he was slumped behind the wheel of the combine. One of the farmhands found him. His heart stopped and he took his last breath doing what he loved."

Palmer choked on a sob, Maureen buried her face in Atta's lap and cried. She felt Atta's hands stroking her hair, attempting to comfort her. She stayed on the floor at Atta's feet for the longest time, and when she finally came up for air, Atta appeared stoic and strong. She reminded her of herself days after she lost Isaac. It was as if she was too numb to feel. "Have you seen him?" Maureen believed they had said their goodbyes during her drive time there. "I'd like to… if it's not too late."

"We waited for you," Palmer said.

"This whole time?" Tears welled up in Maureen's eyes again.

"Yes," Palmer told her. "He was your father, too."

Atta added, "Your Jon Boy would not have wanted it any other way. Now, let's go in there to see him together, as a family."

Maureen got on her feet, while Palmer helped Atta to stand and steady her balance. With Atta in the middle, both girls hooked their arms through hers. This wasn't going to be the hardest thing Maureen ever did. She already buried her son. But this was going to hurt more than she could have ever prepared herself for.

In a sterile room, the shades were drawn, and on a single, white gurney laid a man who never sat still a day in his life. His flannel shirt was buttoned up to the neck, just as he always wore it. Maureen imagined the paramedics had bared his chest when they found him, pouncing on it to find a sign of life in a heart that was more than eight decades old.

Both Palmer and Maureen stood two steps behind Atta, as she approached the man she had spent her entire adulthood living alongside. She reached for his hand. "Oh dear," she choked on a sob. "You rest, my Jon. You've earned it." There was a long pause before she told him, "I hope to join you sooner than later." Her face was tear stained when she turned around. Clearly, she loved him. "I can't see him like this. I want to remember him full of life."

"It's okay, mom," Palmer tried to comfort her, but Atta stiffened.

"Say your goodbyes, girls."

It was a direct, almost unfeeling, order from a mother who still wanted to have some control, and they both did as they were told. Palmer went first. She openly cried, she thanked her father for loving her and being there for her throughout her entire life. Maureen couldn't help but think that was a jab at Atta for abandoning her for six months, but she pushed that thought aside as now was not the time. When it was Maureen's turn, she gently placed both of her hands on his chest and she spoke from her heart. "You were the only father I've ever known. I love you, Jon Boy. Could I ask you for one more favor? Yes, even in death, I need you to help me. Please find Isaac up there, and somehow let me know if he's okay?" Maureen gave in to her tears now, and Palmer held her close, wondering how much grief one family could take. When Atta's girls turned around, she was seated on a chair against the wall, resting her weary body that now sheltered a broken heart.

"We are fortunate to have had this time with him, to say goodbye. It's what he would have wanted," Atta spoke sternly. "He changed his funeral arrangements after we lost our grandboy. He told me that he wanted to be cremated. No lifeless body to view in a casket. He didn't want the three of us to endure that kind of pain again, especially you Reen."

Maureen could have cried again. "For me?"

Atta nodded.

"Told you he loved you more," Palmer quipped, and Maureen smiled through her tears of gratitude for a family that never failed her.

Chapter 11

"You can stay here as long as you want. This farmhouse is your home." Maureen was speaking to Atta while they sat on the front porch with Palmer.

"Or you can leave it behind, if it's too difficult to be here without dad." Palmer cautiously suggested the second option for her mother because she and Maureen had already agreed not to force Atta one way or the other. She had just lost her husband. Rash decision making was said to never be a good thing following a death of a loved one. Although Maureen didn't quite agree. Her husband had left her the same day of their son's funeral, and she too took off to get away from everything familiar. But now she was already back home. She thought of the cottage she rushed out of. Her Keurig was still there, and so were the flowers from Joey. They were likely droopy and wilted by now without proper care. *That figures.* She thought how this was just another piece of significance in her life that was dead.

Atta shook her head. "I am not leaving. This is my home. With or without Jon, I still feel like I belong here. It was typical Atta to know what she wanted, and to voice it — oftentimes stubbornly. Maureen admired that about her, while Palmer typically felt annoyed. It was probably because she shared her mother's headstrong gene.

"We will respect your decision," Maureen supported the woman who raised her. "You will just have to remember not to hesitate to call us if you need help with anything."

"We called you home early from your getaway." There was disappointment in Atta's tone.

"I don't think that could be helped," she defended the unexpected death of her adoptive father.

"Jon didn't want you to leave town anyway," Atta stifled a chuckle. "His actions were a tad extreme to get you back here though."

They all laughed a little together.

"I never would have left if I had known," Maureen spoke seriously.

"We know," Atta reassured her. "I guess you weren't gone long enough for much to change with your well-being and all.

You can always go back, you know?"

Palmer stayed silent. All she could think about was juggling it all alone. Running the newspaper business, and now caring for their recently widowed mother. Not to mention she had a family of her own. She would never throw any of that in Maureen's face. She would just find a way to make it all work.

Maureen shrugged, as if she agreed, as if she had not had time on Great River Road to make connections or have a reason to want to go back. She thought of little Joey in his red baseball cap. And her memory wouldn't allow her to forget being entangled in the sheets with his dad. Back at the cottage, his phone number was on that post-it on the counter.

"I know," was all Maureen said, but the truth was she really didn't know what she was going to do.

Atta stood up slowly, shuffling her Ugg boots on the concrete. "I'm going inside to rest. These past few days have drained me. God knows my body is ready to give out, too."

Palmer started to stand up, but Atta stopped her. "No. You keep sitting. I can manage, I'm not a invalid."

Palmer rolled her eyes in Maureen's direction as she scooted back on her chair again. When the door closed behind Atta, Palmer was quick to speak. "She hates to be needy."

'I'm aware," Maureen noted. "We should be grateful for that. Anyone one else's elderly mother would already have one of us living here."

"Don't speak it," Palmer scolded her, "and don't even think about that as being an option for you."

"I lost my family, Palmer. I did think about Atta needing me here, and how I have nothing holding me back from leaving my own home behind."

"We will work something out when that time comes. I think she would do well at an assisted living center, I mean, as social as she is and all."

"As of now, that option is a hard no for her."

They both agreed on that.

"Are you going back to the cottage? Or, I guess I should ask, do you want to?"

Maureen thought for a moment before she responded. "I left the flowers behind that Joey gave me."

Palmer studied her face. That was a strange answer. "Reen, he's not Isaac…"

"I know." Tears threatened to spill from Maureen's eyes.

"He's just really special. I drove down the hill by the riverbank, and I found their house. I wanted to personally thank them for those flowers."

"How did that work out?"

Maureen laughed. "You would never believe it." Palmer smiled because Maureen was smiling, but she had no idea where this was going. "They were home. Joey invited me inside, I started to decline the offer, thinking that would be awkward, but then Andy encouraged it. We ended up in the backyard watching Joey play basketball."

"The only thing I am taking away from all that you just said is the look on your face when you say their names. I'm worried about this attachment you seem to have formed for that child."

"You probably should be more concerned about the fact that I slept with Andy."

Palmer's jaw dropped. "You did not..."

"I can't believe it either, actually." The expression on Maureen's face was a cross between embarrassed and proud. It was like they were young again and confessing to a one night stand. Maureen went on to explain the wine and cheese, her emotional breakdown, and the impromptu playdate that Joey had at the neighbor's house.

"He got you drunk on purpose!" Palmer immediately formed her own opinion.

"I choose not to believe that," Maureen responded. "He's incredibly good looking. There was a mutual attraction, like sparks from the very beginning, I was feeling needy. We kissed, and then I boldly initiated for more."

"Is this for real?"

"Palmer, it was incredible sex. Everything about Archer and I went stale years ago. Being with Andy was like reigniting a fire in me that had long been extinguished."

"I was joking when I said to get yourself a groundskeeper."

"Call me Atta."

They laughed.

"Can I ask you something?"

"Yes, he was an attentive lover, not a selfish one." In their lingo, that translated to, she orgasmed.

Palmer laughed again. "Not what I was going to ask but go Reen!" They high fived each other from their adjacent rocking chairs. "I will ask this out of love and concern, not judgement. Did you have sex with him to get back at Archer for screwing the slut next door?"

"No," Maureen was quick to answer. "I slept with Andy because I wanted to. He made me forget for a while. I'm sad and grieving and more lost than I've ever felt in my entire life. This was about me."

"What happens now?"

"I don't know. He wrote his number on a post-it, which I left on the kitchen counter at the cottage."

"Why didn't you put his number in your phone?"

Maureen shrugged.

"It's okay if you think you made a mistake. You don't have to date the man."

"He's still married, so am I, for that matter."

"If his marriage is as over as yours, I don't think that's relevant."

"I never said I wanted a relationship. I am too broken to be good for anyone at this stage in my sad life."

"Not true," Palmer reacted. "You have love left to give."

"I'm not interested in falling in love again."

"I never said you had to go out there and date to marry. You deserve to be carefree and have a little fun. Clearly, the party has already started."

They both cackled, and then simultaneously shushed each other as a reminder that Atta was napping and neither of them wanted her to overhear this scandalous conversation. Even though she just might understand.

Chapter 12

Andy was irritable. He told himself to get over Reen Ryan, as she clearly had not wanted to reach out to him. He gave her his number, believing they would see each other again. Clearly, he was wrong. He told himself not to act stalkerish and drive by her cottage, but he did so only once. Her car was not there. At least he knew she was capable of coming and going, and nothing terrible had happened to her. Reen was staying there alone, and he had hoped someone occasionally checked on her. He certainly couldn't be that person. Not after she jilted him.

He knew she had a broken heart. She just lost her child in the worst way. Her husband walked out on her. Life had turned on Reen and left her alone and sad. Andy wanted to help her and be the support system she needed, but she obviously regretted what they did together, and she was not interested in calling him. Again, Andy told himself it would be best if he put her out of his mind.

If he learned anything from their encounter, it was that life was fleeting and unpredictable, and he was no longer interested in living in limbo. Andy hired an attorney to file for a divorce. He knew of a good one. He learned that since his wife abandoned their marriage and was no longer reachable by phone or a mailing address, he could legally end their marriage through a process called divorce by publication. It was tedious and borderline ridiculous, but it was the only way Andy could be set free. Since his attempts to reach her by phone failed, his next step had to be to post a missing person notice in public locations. If that also proved to be unsuccessful, the final step was to search hospital records, obituaries, and jail records. If there was still no trace of his wife, Andy would have to go before a judge to dissolve the marriage from an unresponsive spouse. Andy would also request for the judge to rule in favor of granting him full custody of Joey. It was a somewhat burdensome process, but Andy was determined to do it to be able to move on.

Meanwhile, he had been fielding the questions from Joey, asking when they could see Reen again. Andy suggested they leave it up to chance. Perhaps their paths would cross one more time. Andy certainly hoped so.

Maureen had been back in her house for a matter of days when she felt herself being pulled under the unwavering grief. She stood in front of the open window blinds and looked across the street at her neighbor's house. She had yet to see her husband's vehicle there, and for that she was a tad grateful. He, at the very least, should fly under the radar until they were divorced. She held her phone in her hand now and called Archer. He didn't deserve an advanced warning text; she didn't care if she was interrupting whatever he was doing. His job as an orthopedic surgeon was demanding and time consuming, so Maureen had become accustomed to not contacting him during the workday. She took the chance now and called him.

He answered on the third ring.

"Reen, hi," he spoke with that familiar air of confidence. "Did you get my text about Jon?" He sent it a couple days ago to offer his condolences, as well as a work-related excuse for why he would miss the funeral. Maureen had not replied. She could have said a simple, thank you, but he also could have gone to his father-in-law's funeral out of respect.

"I did, thank you," she said, better late than never.

"How's Atta?"

Reen wondered why he was being so cordial... and chatty.

"She's okay. It's going to be an adjustment for her. It's sad to see one without the other, at least for me it is. I've always known them as a pair." Why was she telling him this? She called with a purpose, and she needed to get to that point. "Listen, um, the reason I called is I've made a decision about the house. I think we should sell it as soon as possible. I also plan to hire an attorney to draw up our divorce papers." She barely took a breath between words. All those changes ahead overwhelmed her.

Archer was silent for a moment on the other end of the phone. "You're making some major decisions."

"Don't say that it's too much too soon. I can't be in this house anymore, not without Isaac." She confirmed how he felt as well.

"I miss that kid."

His words tore at her soul. She ached to share this level of pain with someone who understood. But she also knew that she and Archer would never share anything ever again.

"I have to move," she told him again, "and a divorce is the next logical thing considering the naked fun you're having with our neighbor." The truth didn't sting as much as it should have. Perhaps that was because of what she did with Andy Perry. Now they had both broken their marriage vows.

Archer ignored her last comment.

"I will contact a real estate agent, and I guess we should both hire a divorce attorney. Reen, this will be amicable. Whatever you want in the house is yours. I mean, I would like to divvy Isaac's things."

Reen never thought of that. She wanted to be so quick to box up everything and get out of there, she had forgotten that also meant going into Isaac's room and sorting through his things.

"Of course," was all she could muster the strength to say.

"I'll be in touch then," Archer initiated the end of their conversation that was both genuine and awkward.

"Okay, thanks."

"Reen?" He caught her before she ended their call. "Take care of yourself."

"Yes, you too."

Chapter 13

Their house on Old Trenton Road sold within two weeks. Maureen was consumed with packing and putting things in storage, and even leaving a few things at the farmhouse in her old bedroom. She cautiously clarified to Atta that she was not moving back. She was a grownup and needed to live on her own. That same day, Maureen got a call from the owner of the cottage, reminding her that her one-month lease was almost expired. It was as if his call was meant to be. The man had no idea that Maureen was not currently staying there. Or maybe he did? In any case, Maureen's request to rent the cottage on Great River Road for the next six months was granted. She wanted to go back, she hoped to anyway, and now she had a reason. Her home was sold, and she realized she had not been able to give that space at the cottage a chance. It was serene, and as soon as she settled things with her old life, she was anticipating going back there. Even if it was only for a little while.

"Are you sure you're okay?"

Maureen was walking through the main floor of her empty two-story home. It looked even more spacious without furniture. Her memory took her back to the day she and Archer moved in. She was eight and a half months pregnant with Isaac. There was so much promise ahead. She remembered feeling as if her life was just beginning, that the best years were still ahead of her. Maureen held her phone to her ear as she answered Palmer's question.

"I am okay. Archer is on his way."

While the entire house was completely vacant, the door to Isaac's room remained closed and his room was left untouched. Today was the day they agreed to sort through their boy's things and move everything out. Archer was bringing a truck to haul the furniture, but neither one of them were even sure where they wanted it to go yet.

Palmer was calling from the newspaper office, where she had apologized profusely for not being able to get away. Maureen certainly understood being on deadline. What she didn't tell Palmer was that she also had been considering leaving their business. She would buy out her half so Palmer would not feel the loss. They would both, however, grieve their dream of running that company together until they were older and ready for retirement. This wasn't a definite decision for Maureen, but it had potential to happen. Again, she warned herself of changing too much too fast in her life. And that was why she didn't mention anything yet.

The front door opened and in walked Archer. Because there was no furniture, Maureen was standing in the middle of the living room when he walked into what used to be their home. She stared at him at first. He was wearing black joggers and a gray long-sleeve t-shirt. She didn't recognize the gray ballcap or two-toned black and gray sneakers on his feet. For a moment she felt like saying something snarky. Shopping had been the last thing on her mind since their son died. She refrained, and said, "hi," instead.

He nodded, and she knew by looking at him that his emotions were in his throat. This was going to be a difficult day.

"Everything is gone," she said of the things they used to share in that house. Archer had already gotten his personal things. They agreed to divvy up some furniture and donated others. All the kitchen stuff, Maureen kept. Archer's talent was in the operating room as a skilled surgeon. He didn't know the first thing about cooking or doing much else around the house. Maureen remembered her adoptive father once calling him a pretty boy, and that wasn't inaccurate.

"I guess we better get started in his room then," Archer cautiously spoke.

"This move, and selling the house so quickly seemed like the right thing to do..." she hesitated, "but having to rush our way through Isaac's things so soon somehow seems wrong."

"We don't have to rush, Reen. We can do this all day, or even all night long. Whatever it takes. I don't have anywhere else to be."

Her mind flashed to Jamie, right across the damn street. She was likely on her front porch looking their way through binoculars to see what they were doing together. Maureen pushed that image and her from her mind. She did appreciate Archer's compassion. She hadn't seen that person in years. They somehow became strangers to each other throughout their broken marriage.

"I appreciate you. I mean, I don't think I could do this alone."

Archer reached for her hand, and she was okay with that as they walked together, up the stairway, to their son's bedroom one last time.

It was Archer who reached for the door handle first. Maureen watched him push it open. She followed him inside. She stopped immediately after stepping over the threshold. The room carried his scent. It still lingered there even though he was gone. She took in all the air she could, inhaling him. Archer had tears streaming down his face already. Maureen's emotions were in check. She wanted to say that she had changed her mind. The sale of the house was off. How could she leave now? Not when this room somehow preserved more than Isaac's memory. Maureen was stoic as she looked around the room. His queen-sized bed was neatly made with a navy duvet. His four pillows were stacked high at the headboard. His dresser top was full of clutter. The chair in the corner had clothes strewn across the back of it. Her eyes continued to scan the room until she focused on the double panel closet doors. Her breath caught. Her mind flashed to the scene she saw when she got home from the newspaper office late that afternoon. Isaac had taken the bus home an hour earlier. Maureen sprinted up the stairs, calling his name. When she opened his bedroom door, she dropped to her knees. Those closet doors were wide open. The chair in the corner had been moved. From the doorframe, she saw her son, the length of the rope, the noose. She felt herself beginning to lose consciousness then from the shock of what she saw. Instead, she fought to get to her feet, she forced that chair closer to him, shoving it overtop the berber carpet. She stood on it, balancing while struggling to free him. Yelling, screaming, crying out her boy's name. Finally, his body dropped to the floor. He was free. Free for what? Maureen cried. Free for her call to 911, for her to beat on his chest and pump air into him from her mouth to his? He was already gone. She bent over his body and sobbed until she nearly threw up. Then, she called Archer and an ambulance.

Archer stood close to her near the doorway, knowing she was reliving her worst nightmare. She saw him staring at her with concern in his eyes. She came back to reality then. "It's best if we do this," she meant sorting through his things and leaving the space where he left this world behind. There was no way she could see this room, day after day. "The not knowing why haunts me though." Archer stepped away from her. He was suddenly closed off again, just like he had been for the days surrounding the funeral.

"I'd like to have his tennis racket," Archer said, walking over to the far corner of the room and lifting the racket into his hands. He taught his son how to play, and he had been playing this school year as a freshman at Highland High School, where he already ranked in the top three. By the time he was a senior, he would own the top rank, he told them at the beginning of the school year, just several weeks ago. He had life goals, short-term and long-term. He didn't aspire to be a surgeon like his father or a journalist like his mother. Just in the last year or so, Isaac had talked about wanting to study psychiatry. The mind is our most powerful tool, he once told Maureen, and she looked back now and wondered what he really meant. She asked him then, and his reply had almost been beyond her comprehension. She still remembered his exact words, and she wondered why now they were coming to her. "Responses of the nervous system happen below the level of conscious awareness in the survival brain." Maureen had completely forgotten this. She used to refer to her son as a brainiac, but those specific words meant something to him then. Was he fighting with his conscious, struggling to survive? How long had he been in that kind of hell? And how could she not have seen it?

"I asked if it would be okay if I take his racket."

Maureen snapped out of her thoughts. "Yes, sure. He would want you to have it."

They started to open drawers and sort and make piles. Maureen wanted to take all of his clothing, but she knew Archer deserved to have some too. He chose three of his hoodies, and his watch, and told Maureen she could have the rest. Maureen sat on the bed with those three hoodies he asked for. She intended to fold them and set them aside. Instead, she covered her lap with two and brought the third to her face. She buried her senses in the material.

"It's so hard to let go," Archer heard her say.

"I know. It's unfair that we even have to feel our way through this pain for the rest of our lives." Archer's words touched her. Again, someone else completely understood the depth of her pain from this loss. "I'll never forgive myself," she heard the words that he spat into the air.

"Why would you say something like that?"

"I'm his father. I should have paid more attention, seen the signs."

"Were there signs?" Maureen's tone was borderline angry, and she didn't know who she wanted to direct that anger and frustration toward. Archer? Isaac? Or herself for feeling just as guilty as her soon-to-be ex-husband.

He shrugged.

"I didn't see them either," she added, with a sudden calmness to her demeanor.

Maureen saw Archer fiddling with the strings on the tennis racket, which he had picked up again.

"There are some pictures that I wanted him to send to me from his phone, the ones from his latest match." Archer had been in surgery, and Maureen had arrived late, following an interview for the newspaper. Another parent had taken some photos and shared them. "I haven't cracked the code." She really hadn't tried much either. Just his birthdate and a few other things that came to mind. Nothing was the correct passcode. "I will share those photos when I do."

"Maybe leave well enough alone?"

"What? Not even try to get into his phone to preserve the memories that are what's left of our son? That's too much to ask."

"I didn't mean that," was all he said, and Maureen chose to let it go, right after Archer said he always thought his son was the best tennis player this side of the Mississippi River.

Four hours passed. They had the bed taken apart, the dresser emptied, and the closet was the last place they were working. Archer was trying to be the one to step into it and take things out, and just hand them to Maureen. He knew this space was haunting her and would for the rest of her life. The expression on her face went blank again, as he was about to say he thought that was the last of it.

Maureen told herself to be strong, they were almost through with all of this. She felt her heart rate increase and the tears suddenly stung in her eyes. She dropped to her knees, just like she had that day. She looked up and Archer had gripped her shoulders to keep her from landing too hard. The moment she looked at him, she saw their son. Isaac looked so much like him, and at fourteen he was becoming a man and those features from his father were more prominent. For years upon years, she saw Archer in their son. As a baby, as a toddler, as a little boy, and as a teenager. And now, she was seeing their son in his father — because the child was dead.

She cried out Isaac's name. Archer was now down on his knees with her. "Noooo! Isaac! Nooo!" Sobs followed the screams. Hard, gut-wrenching sobs. Archer didn't let go of his grip on her. He also could not contain his own emotions. He openly cried with her, especially the moment she fell against his chest and went limp in his arms. Her strength to get through this day was utterly drained.

It was a while before either of them spoke again. They made their way in and out of that bedroom, many trips up and down the stairway and outside to their separate vehicles. When the last things were taken out of Isaac's room, they stood in the hallway. Maureen internally debated on whether or not she wanted the door to be left open or closed again. It seemed silly, but it mattered to her.

"Do you think we should close the door? I don't think I can. Will you?" She was rambling, and Archer just stood there thinking and wishing he had the right words to say or the best thing to do to give her closure.

And then he did. He believed he knew what to do.

"I think we should leave it open," Archer suggested. "Maybe that could be our way of not trying to force closure on this. I don't see us ever getting past or getting over this loss or closing the door on our past with him. This open door, left this way for us right now, will be our way of telling him that our hearts will always be open for him with no protective barriers. We will never stop feeling this pain, freely loving him, and he will live on in us."

Maureen covered her mouth with her hand and nodded in agreement. When she was finally capable of speaking, after she regained some composure, she said, "Thank you for saying all of that in the most heartfelt way."

They both stared at that open door longer than they meant to before heading down the stairway one last time. Again, they ended up standing in the middle of the spacious living room.

"We could order pizza or something," Archer's suggestion was impromptu. "I'm sure you're hungry."

She smiled. "We should both go." She refrained from adding, *our separate ways.*

Archer obliged. "Reen? Can I ask you something?"

"Okay" she waited.

"Do you think if we had tried harder to make us work… you know, to love each other more and really see each other like we once did… do you think that would have mattered? Would that have saved Isaac?"

Maureen didn't know where this was coming from other than the intense emotions they were put through all day long. "I think our son had a mind of his own. I don't want to believe that we caused him to give up."

Archer sighed, and then reluctantly said, "I will try to believe that, too."

Reen had so many questions and her reporter instinct told her to get the answers, to never give up until she had them. But as a worn out, grief-stricken mother, she was beginning to give up on ever knowing the truth. Maybe she should search for acceptance instead?

"I wonder something," Archer added. "I will ask you this once and if it's a hard no, I'll turn around and never look back." Maureen listened with a puzzled look on her face. "What if we were to try again to make our marriage work? Would that give our son some peace wherever he is?"

Maureen took a deep breath before she spoke to her husband. "That's a hard no."

His lips broke into a smile, and he said, "Okay, you're right," before he turned on his heels to open the front door for them.

And this time it was Maureen who called him back. "Archer?"

He turned around.

"It's not our fault."

He had tears in his eyes when they parted ways.

Chapter 14

It occurred to Maureen as she drove away from their home, one last time, that if it weren't for the cottage on Great River Road, she would be homeless. Extending the lease on that was probably the best decision she made in a while. It wasn't a permanent home, not even long-term, and it was far from being local, but it was going to work for her. She could feel it. She actually missed it.

Before she left town, she stopped at the farmhouse to drop off most of what she had packed into her trunk and backseat. She carried each bin and all the bags into her old bedroom. She stacked everything along the wall, as Atta leaned against the doorframe and watched.

"What will you do with our boy's things?" It was a heartbreaking question.

Maureen didn't know the answer. The last thing she wanted to do was give up anything too soon. Donations could wait. All of Isaac's things had sentimental value to her now. "I'll hold onto most of it," she answered truthfully.

Atta silently accepted her decision, but then she had another question. 'If you do not want to stay here, where will you go?" Without Jon Boy, the farmhouse was another difficult place for Maureen to be. She actually wished that Atta would have wanted to sell the house, just like she had her own. To avoid more pain.

"Back to the cottage. It's only an hour away and I can go back and forth when I'm needed."

"I, of course, want you to come back whenever you feel like it," Atta began, "but don't put anyone else first except for Reen. Are you hearing me? Take this time to breathe and contemplate what it is you want out of life. Life…" Atta paused, as she appeared to be overcome with emotion, "has not been very kind to you. It's time that you make your own happiness. Don't be crushed by your hardships. Do not let the pain win. You deserve the world, my girl. I have thought that from the moment I met you as a child."

Maureen walked over to the woman who played the role of a mother to her for four decades. She never called her mom, but she loved her every ounce as if she were the woman who gave her life. Atta's body appeared frail, but she had some strength in those arms as Maureen embraced her before she said goodbye for now.

Maureen had not even made it halfway to her destination and her phone was ringing. She checked to see who was calling and then put Palmer on speaker phone.

"Where are you going?" Those were the first words out of Palmer's mouth.

"Are you tracking me on Life 360?"

Palmer was surprised there was laughter in her tone. Today had to have been a heartbreaking day, and Atta just called her to report that Maureen was leaving town again. "No, but that's not a bad idea."

"Let me guess, you've talked to Atta in the last hour?"

"Somebody had to tell me."

"I would have, I was just letting the deadline pass."

"You didn't have to leave the moment you packed up Isaacs's room."

"I was homeless, so yeah I kind of did."

"There's the farmhouse or my house."

"I want a place of my own."

"How long are you going to be able to call the cottage your home?"

"At least six months."

Palmer was quiet on the opposite end of the phone.

"I'll be back and forth. I don't plan to use it as a hideaway," Maureen attempted to reassure her.

"Reen, I realize that you need time, I do. I have no right to push or anything, but I need to know what's going through your head with the paper." She was referring to their joint business, The Highland Times.

Maureen sighed a little as she kept her eyes on the windy road in front of her. "I don't feel passionate about it anymore," she admitted. "I guess I didn't know how to tell you. So much about my life will never be the same again. A part of me wonders how much more I will have to, or want to, let go of."

"You have to stop doing this," Palmer reacted. "The newspaper was our shared dream, we wanted to do this together. You can't keep walking away from things that matter to you."

"Like what?" Maureen immediately felt defensive. "My only child? He gave up. My marriage? We don't love each other anymore. My house? It's not a home without my family in it. Don't get me started on Jon Boy and the farmhouse not feeling the same anymore."

At first, Palmer didn't know what to say, but it was her nature to be blunt. "No one is hurting for you as much as I am," she began. "Just stop running so I can catch up with you and help you."

"I need to do this right now. Yes, the cottage is an escape, and I know I cannot stay there forever. I just need time. I know you're swamped running things alone—"

"It's not about that," Palmer partially lied. "It's you, saying you're ready to quit. Reen, remember who the hell you are. You don't give up."

"Easy for you to say," Maureen shot back, "when everything has not been taken away from your life."

"That's not fair."

Maureen backed off. She knew better than to say something so selfish. Palmer loved Isaac like her own. And Palmer was also the one who lost *her* father. Maureen had only borrowed him since she was nine years old.

"I'm sorry," she heard herself say.

"I know," Palmer's words were just as sincere.

"I just need a minute."

"Take what you need and call me later."

Chapter 15

Before going back to the cottage to, once again, settle in, Maureen stopped at the Grafton Market to stock up on a few things she knew she would immediately need. What was left in the refrigerator and on the counter from a few weeks ago would be of no use to her. She just wanted to get back to the cottage, unpack, and be alone. Even the idea of cooking did not appeal to her, so that's when she decided to make one more stop. She called The Loading Dock to place an order for fish tacos. She didn't have much of an appetite in the last few weeks, so when something appealed to her, she chased after it.

Maureen was in good spirits as she entered the riverfront restaurant and bar. The place was busy, as she made her way toward the bar to pick up her order. While she waited a minute to be helped, Maureen scanned her surroundings. The indoor fireplace was lit, even though the November weather had not changed from chilly to cold yet. As she looked around at everyone dining and simply being together, she felt a tug at her heart. She was alone. Not by choice, but because her life had been stripped from her in the worst way. Before she allowed herself to sink too deep into despair in public, she zeroed in on a couple seated a short distance from the fireplace. She caught her breath when she saw a brunette with striking features, sitting across from Andy Perry.

She hadn't thought about him in a while. Or maybe she had, but she didn't want to admit it to herself. In any case, she wondered if that woman was his wife. For Joey's sake, that would be best. She caught herself trying to read Andy's body language. Was he comfortable with her? If they were married, of course he was. If this was someone he was newly dating, good for him, she thought, but didn't sincerely mean that. The fact that Maureen was staring and reading way too much into what Andy was doing was a problem. What she needed to do was get her food and go. But, just as a waitress approached her about her order, Andy's head turned. And he saw her.

Maureen looked away, and she hoped that sudden reaction had not been obvious. She turned her back, paid for her food order, and just as she turned around, planning to dart away without looking in his direction again, he was there. Right there. Standing in her path.

"Reen, hi. I'm surprised to see you here."

"Hi," she tried to speak nonchalantly. "Likewise." There was no reason to have flashbacks of getting naked with him. It was the craziest, most impromptu thing she had ever done in her entire life. It was passionate and liberating... and she was embarrassed at the thought of it now. And besides, Andy had clearly moved on. He had a date. Or a wife who returned to pick up where they left off. If that indeed was her over there watching Maureen right now, she really needed to go. Now.

"Is this awkward?" he brought it up.

"No, of course not," she lied.

"I just wanted to see how you're doing."

She really hoped he would not bring up how she never called him. She was certain that post-it was on the counter at the cottage right where she left it a few weeks ago. So much had happened since then. Once again, her life had ended up on its rear end. She still was not certain Jon Boy's death had completely sunk into her heart. The funeral itself was too soon to process following Isaac's. She respected the fact that 'How Great Thou Art' was Jon Boy's favorite church hymn, but it tore her apart to hear it at her son's funeral Mass, and again for Jon Boy.

"I'm okay," she answered.

"Good." She was holding her take-out food. He was rocking on his heels with his thumbs in the front pockets of his denim.

"I should let you get back to your date."

Andy glanced behind him at the woman sitting at their table alone now. "Her?"

Maureen nodded.

Andy grinned. "Reen Ryan? Are you jealous?"

She smirked. "Um, no. Why would I be jealous?" She paused, and then thought, what the hell, she was going to ask for clarification. "Is she your wife?"

"No, she's not. That woman over there is two things to me." Here we go, Maureen thought, as she suspected *lover* as being one of the two. "She's my attorney— and my little sister."

"Your sister?" That would explain the gorgeousness.

Andy nodded. "Yes. She has been helping me with the tedious task of getting a divorce. I owed her dinner for that."

Maureen's eyes widened.

"She didn't come back." He referred to his wife, or now ex-wife. "I can explain it sometime, what it's called, and how it works." The bottom line was he was divorced and the woman he was having dinner with was his sister. Maureen tried to remain neutral about all of this.

"For your sake, the closure is good," she noted, "but how's Joey?"

"I've explained this the best way I know how to a five-year-old. He's adjusting." Andy wanted to say 'he misses you… and so do I' … but he didn't want to scare her off. Her walls were clearly back up. He still believed she was uninterested in getting to know him better. The whole idea of that statement was comical considering they had skipped a few important steps and already gone to bed together.

"I miss him," she said, and Andy smiled at her. "I actually just got back in town," she confessed. She wasn't sure what it was about him, but she wanted to confide in him about things. "I've been gone for three weeks."

"Why? Was it because of what we—" He calculated that it had been that long since he was waiting for her to call.

"No," she stopped where his thoughts were going. "Jon," she stopped herself from saying Boy. He didn't know those details of her life. "My adoptive father died suddenly. He was eighty-three, still farming some. His heart gave out while puttering around in a tractor. It was too late when they found him." She held her own as she spoke. It was a sad story, another great loss in her life, but sometimes she just felt hardened from it all.

Andy reached for her. He touched her forearm. "I'm sorry. I didn't know." That explained why she never called him.

"There was no way you could have known."

"Reen, look, I know your food is getting cold…"

"And your attorney-at-law sister is waiting."

He chuckled. "Can I see you again sometime?"

She nodded. "Sure."

He waited.

She started to step aside and spoke at the same time. "I still have that neon yellow post-it. It's been on my counter at the cottage for weeks."

Andy now had a solid explanation for why Maureen didn't reach out to him, so he allowed himself to feel hopeful, once again, as she walked away.

Chapter 16

Maureen entered the cottage feeling different this time. The space was familiar. The quiet was welcomed. That last time she was there, she feared what being alone would do to her. Would she think too much? Cry too easily? Ever get out of bed? This time, she was searching for peace a little less fiercely. She just wanted to exist and simply be in the moment. First, she saw the wilted flowers in a vase at the center of the kitchen table. It made her sad to think she wasn't here to enjoy them. The peach and the orange roses, each symbolized gratitude and happiness. There was one peach rose that caught her eye. Of the six flowers, it was less wilted, and there was life. Maureen couldn't explain it. She lifted it from the rest. It was a survivor among the others that had long died. She was going to keep this one and dry it out and press it so she would forever be reminded of Joey's kindness and to always look for something to be grateful for in her life. No matter what.

Maureen turned away from the table, with the single rose in her hand, and she spotted the post-it on the counter. Would she finally log Andy's number into her phone? *Maybe later.* She smiled as she thought of bumping into him the moment she returned to town. *Thank goodness he was only with his sister.*

Maureen managed to unpack both suitcases soon after she arrived this time. She was getting things done, puttering around the cottage when she heard her cell phone ringing in the kitchen. When she got to it, she wasn't surprised to see it was Palmer calling.

"Hey there," Maureen greeted her.

"Settling in your new home?"

"Temporary home," Maureen corrected her.

"I'm not sure how to go about telling you this other than to just say it."

Damn it. "Now what happened?" Maureen had about enough of her life spiraling out of control.

"Do you have Isaac's phone with you?"

"I do. Why?" Maureen was impatient for whatever it was that Palmer was trying to tell her.

"Reese can help you with the passcode." Reese was Palmer and Jake's oldest daughter. She was three years old when Isaac was born, and he was like a real, live baby doll for her. Palmer and Maureen wanted their kids to grow up close, and they did. Palmer's twins were fifteen and only a year older than Isaac.

"Reese knows Isaac's passcode?" She never even thought about asking the girls. The truth was, she had not been desperate to get into his phone yet. More than anything, she felt unprepared for what she might find.

"Apparently she has been struggling with staying loyal to Isaac. Phones are private, you know. She's worried you'll be upset with her for waiting this long to tell you."

"Not at all. You hug that sweet girl for me until I can," Maureen reacted.

"Remember when Reese was little and she couldn't say Isaac, so she said Zac?"

Maureen smiled. "I think she still called him that occasionally." This was what she wanted. Memories. Keep them coming about her son. It was all she had left to hold onto.

"It's ZAC600. All caps."

"That's far from my guesses. I did try six a few different ways. It's always been his favorite number."

"Reen?"

"Hmm?"

"Take your time with this. Sign in when you're ready. I can even come up there if you want me to sometime."

"I do feel like I have been putting this off. I mean, it was Archer who felt the urgency to get into his phone. Maybe not so much anymore, I don't know."

"It's a hard step, Reen."

"Thank you. I'll be okay."

Palmer hoped with everything she had for that to be true, because she wasn't sure how much more one person could take. When Maureen ended their call, she found Isaac's phone in her purse, and then put it on the charger in the kitchen. She was buying herself just a little more time.

Chapter 17

ZAC600

With her thumbs, Maureen typed the passcode to Isaac's phone. She sat very still in the middle of the sofa in the cottage's small living room. She could hear her own pulse pounding in her ears. She wrapped herself in the blanket she brought with her from home, because it was Isaac's favorite too. They shared it, but often teasingly accused each other of hogging it.

On his lock screen, there was a photo of him playing tennis, in the middle of a serve, showing off his proper serve stance that he had mastered at nine years old. He was a good-looking boy. Maureen traced her index finger over his face. She inhaled a deep breath and opened his phone to the home screen. She would eventually read all the text messages. First, she opened his last exchange with her. It was that afternoon when she was still at the newspaper, and he took the bus home from school. She always made him check in with her once he was off the bus and had a block and a half to walk to their house.

She noticed he had texted her at 3:35 that day. All he said was, *Home.* And Maureen's reply was, *Good. I will be there in about an hour.* She remembered she was finishing an article. At the time, it was important. It never even crossed her mind to tell her son that *she loved him, she was proud of him, she would leave right that minute to spend some time with him.* That's not the way life worked. It's human nature to get caught up in normalcy, a routine. Unexpected loss was the cruelest kind.

She clicked on another text exchange. This one was between Isaac and his dad. The last one was to Isaac from Archer. It said, *We need to talk about this.* There was no response from Isaac to that plea. The messages before were a little puzzling to Maureen. It was mainly Archer doing the messaging. Some were his typical… *great game today… keep working hard on that serve, it's so close to perfection.* Maureen rolled her eyes a bit. Archer was hard on his son, always being overly critical. The damn serve was flawless for the last five years. One of the most recent texts caught Maureen's eye. *I know you have a picture. Trash it. I mean it.* Again, there was no reply from Isaac.

Maureen remembered Archer telling her the last time they were together, taking apart their son's room, that he didn't want her to figure out the passcode, *to leave well enough alone.*

She kept searching through his phone.

The exchanges with his friends were normal teenage interactions. The fact that Isaac was well-liked, and had friends at school, only added to the shock and devastation when he took his own life. After some scrolling, Maureen moved on. She still felt as if she was being intrusive and somehow invading her son's privacy. She had to get that notion out of her mind because this was all she had left of her son.

She moved on to the notes section in his phone.

At the top, he had a note pinned. It was titled, *To Mom.*

Her heart sank. She was afraid of what she was about to read. What if Archer was right and she should just leave well enough alone? What if she sank to an irreversible low after reading his words, knowing she can never confront him because he will never be real to her again? What if the truth was best left uncovered? Maureen could feel it in her soul that she was about to find out why Isaac left this world, and her, behind.

Hi Mom,

If you are reading this, I am already gone.

Ever since I was a child, I've known I would not grow old. I knew I would not wait for the day when God would say my time was up here on earth. I wanted to be in control of my own fate. It's a strange feeling, and I am sure it's awful for you to know this now. I never told you because I didn't want you or dad to freak out. It's nothing you could have prevented. It's a battle I've had within my own body since I was old enough to realize what I was feeling. I don't know how to be happy. I tried, but I can't. I'm incapable. Sometimes I was almost there, almost happy, but it never lasted. I always wanted a sibling so I would not have to feel as lonely. I used to wish for parents with less demanding jobs so you and dad would spend more time with me. I didn't care that we had a big house and a lot of money. I wanted a simpler life. I love playing tennis, I was better than good enough, but I was not the best yet. Maybe those top ranks would have come in time, but I ran out of time.

You used to say my behavior was just me being a teenager. I would hear you explain me this way. But I knew better. I knew how I felt inside my head. My mind would never rest long enough to leave me alone. Some days were better than others. I could talk more, laugh more, sleep well, and I even ate normally. Then, something would happen to me, inside my head again. It was like a switch turned off, and I was left with darkness. Each time, I sank deeper, but no one noticed. I accepted that there would come a day when I would not make it back up from this deep dark hole. I was not getting out of this, out of my own head, alive.

Mom, promise me something. Promise me that you will not blame yourself. You were the best mom for me. I believe that with all my heart. I want you to be happy. I know you and dad only stayed together for me. I know you never loved each other, not that I could see. Find a new path, mom. You deserve better.

As for me, I am confident that I will be at peace when you are finally reading my words.

Thank you for loving me. I loved you back. I only wish I had been able to learn to love myself.

Find happiness.

Love,

Isaac

Maureen's thoughts were spiraling. She couldn't cry. She couldn't scream. She sat strangely still under the blanket that once comforted her son, a boy who she never really knew at all. His words were sad and alarming and somewhat accusatory. Even if he did not mean to place blame, she and Archer were his parents and somewhere along the way they failed their son.

Maureen thought of her own life... and how she had always felt like happiness was a thing meant for everyone else, except for her. Almost was too big a word. She felt it everywhere. She was almost home— with Palmer's family. She was almost happy being Maureen. Almost content with her choices, her life. Almost, but not quite.

What if she had passed on some type of defective gene to her son? He, too, never felt like a whole person. He was just going through the motions. It pained her to think that she could have understood him, if she had known. Instead, they both covered up their pain and carried on. Until Isaac couldn't anymore.

She opened another 'note.' This one was for Archer.

Dad,

I wasn't going to leave you a letter. I am so angry with you. I don't think you deserve my words, or a goodbye from me. My mother deserved better than you. You are a coward for what you are doing to her, and for making me stay quiet. A real man would have owned his mistakes, and bowed out gracefully when his marriage was no longer working. My mom doesn't need you. She is strong and independent all on her own.

I said I was angry with you, but I don't hate you.

I'll always be your son, the best tennis player on this side of the Mississippi.

Love,

Isaac

Maureen was dumbfounded. Isaac clearly had known about Archer's affair with their neighbor. Or perhaps there had been someone else before her? The sad truth was, Maureen didn't even care that Archer had cheated on her. What hurt her was knowing their son had known and it had crushed him because he was worried about her.

She thought back to the text messages she had searched earlier. Archer's last words to his son were: *We need to talk about this. I know you have a picture. Trash it.*

Maureen closed out of the notes and opened the photo gallery now. If there was a picture, she was going to find it. It didn't take much scrolling through the abundance of tennis photos, the random screen shots, and there it was. Taken from the upstairs window of Isaac's bedroom. The view was directly across the street. The image was of his father and another woman. They were in the open doorway of the neighbor's home. Jamie's back was parallel to the doorframe and Archer's body was pressed against hers. Maureen zoomed in. They were heavily kissing.

She chided Archer for being careless and stupid in plain sight, in a direct view of his son. It pained her to know that Isaac had been forced to keep quiet. She would have reassured him that she was okay. She could handle it. Maureen would have done so many things different, given the chance. Especially knowing what she knew now.

She was so angry. Without thinking, she pulled up Archer's name on her phone, attached the incriminating photo, and sent it.

You son of a bitch, she thought to herself. *Not because of what you did to me, but what your actions did to our son.* She wanted Archer to suffer right now when he saw that photo, the one he so desperately wanted his son to delete, the one he frantically tried to get to first on his son's phone after he was gone.

A reply from Archer came through almost immediately.

Blame me. I already do.

This time, Maureen chose to be passive aggressive and leave well enough alone when she never replied to his message. She just went back to searching through her son's phone, now on his social media accounts. Those posts and those pictures made her feel connected to him. Her boy. He would forever be her boy, no matter where he was. And tonight, the tears never came.

Chapter 18

Surprisingly, she slept. Yet, Maureen woke up feeling odd. Was this peace? Or was she numb? Some of what she relived in her mind from last night felt like an awful dream. At the same time, she reminded herself that she knew the truth and she would no longer have to live with the uncertainty and the unanswered questions.

Did that lessen the pain? No.

She wanted to call Palmer, but she stopped herself. Everything was on her lately. The newspaper. Atta now living without Jon Boy. She also had her own family to keep afloat. She would bother Palmer later, but right now she couldn't bring herself to unload on her.

Maureen held the post-it in her hand.

Find happiness. Those were her son's words to her. She thought of Andy and Joey… and the way she felt each time she was with them. Even a brief run-in at the restaurant had left her heart smiling.

She set the post-it back down on the counter.

She needed to focus on herself.

She stared at the number anyway and logged it into her phone.

A second later, she sent him a text. She was overcome with the mindset of she had to live. She could not lose herself in this grief any more than she already had.

Hi, it's me.

Andy saw the text come through without a caller ID. He knew immediately. He saw something in those few words that made him question if she was at a low point, or the complete opposite and feeling daring and giddy? Even at the restaurant he could see the sadness in her eyes. She couldn't hide that from him. As strange as it seemed, he could read so much about her already. He proceeded cautiously to send a reply.

Reen. Good to hear from you. All okay over there?

He could tell that she was not yet replying because he didn't see the bubble with the three dots on his phone which signified someone was texting at the moment. Andy put his phone back in the cupholder in the console between him and Joey. He was driving him to school.

"Who was that, dad? Work?"

Andy shook his head. "No, it was Reen."

Joey smiled. "I like her dad. I want to see her again."

"Me too," Andy felt a flutter in his heart as he shared his son's wishes.

Once Andy had dropped off Joey, he began to take his route to work. And that's when his phone rang. It was the same number. He picked up after that first ring. "Good morning." He still feared that something was wrong, but he didn't want to overreact if not.

"I tried compiling a text, but I don't know what to say," she confessed, a little nervously.

"It's okay," he told her. "Sometimes a phone call, to hear someone's voice in your ear, is way better."

She sighed. She wasn't going to cry. But there was something about him. Or maybe her emotions rising had something to do with the fact that he was the first person she actually spoke aloud to since last night when she uncovered the truth about her son.

Her silence worried Andy. "Hey, listen. I just dropped off Joey at school. You got any coffee in that cottage? I could swing by."

"I have coffee," she choked on her words a little, trying to push down the lump rising in her throat. "But don't you need to get to work?"

"I think the boys can handle piecing together a roof without me."

She laughed a little.

"Reen?"

"Yeah?"

"I'm now headed your way."

"I don't even know how you like your coffee."

"Just black."

"You're easy," she teased, and suddenly she sounded a little more like herself again. Or at least she was trying to overcome the sadness that he heard in her voice the moment she called him.

"I don't want to be a bother," he teased back.

"I think that's the other way around. I'm the needy one interrupting your schedule."

"What if I told you that I like to be needed?"

She smiled. "I'd say see you soon."

Andy accelerated his vehicle to get to her.

Because Maureen knew Andy was on his way to her, she ran to the back of the cottage and looked in the bathroom mirror. Her blonde hair was pulled up high on her head in a messy bun. Her teeth were brushed, her face was washed and makeup free. She wore a pair of black leggings and an oversized heather grey sweatshirt. Her bare feet were cold, but before she could grab a pair of socks from her bedroom drawer, she heard a knock on the cottage door. She went to him right away.

When she opened the door, he stood there in jeans, work boots, and a red polo shirt with the *Perry Roofing* logo embroidered on the left side of his broad chest. "I'm here for a cup of coffee," he said softly.

She stepped back. "Come in."

He followed her into the kitchen. He waited for her to pour two cups of coffee and invite him to sit down at the table with her. She set the coffee mugs on the table but never sat down. She folded her arms across her chest, and he stepped toward her. He reached for both her elbows, taking one in each of his hands. "Hey, forget the coffee for a minute. Talk to me."

She nodded with tears in her eyes. Those were the damn tears that should have surfaced last night when she was alone. Instead, she felt more vulnerable now with him. "I know the passcode to my son's phone. One of Palmer's girls shared it with me. I was able to take a look last night."

Andy listened raptly. He hated knowing she was alone for that. He wanted to comfort her so bad, he ached.

"There were letters. One for me. One for his dad. There was a picture."

"Did any of that give you the answers you need?" Andy interrupted to ask that pertinent question.

She nodded and began to explain that her son hid some underlying feelings throughout his life, he clearly battled with himself until the end. "He was never truly happy. He was more like me than I ever realized," she added after she told Andy about the letter Isaac had written to her.

"What do you mean?" Andy prodded.

"All my life I've recognized that feeling of being almost enough... but I was never completely whole." Andy rubbed the palms of his hands over her forearms as she spoke.

"I wish the two of you could have talked about the feelings you shared alike," he offered.

"So do I, more than you know. But I see now that Isaac was trying to protect me... from a lot of things. He knew about his dad's affair."

"That's heavy for a kid to carry."

"I agree. I just wish things were different. I could have told him that I would be okay if his dad and I got a divorce. I think he believed that, though. He called me strong and independent."

"You're not angry?' Andy asked her.

"I don't know how I feel. I have moments of anger, yes. I am mad that my son is dead, and I am mad at him for it. I am not terribly upset about Archer, but I do hate that Isaac knew."

"How can you not blame Archer for his part in this?" Andy didn't want to say that his father's deception could have been what pushed Isaac over that final edge, It wasn't his place to suggest that though.

"Maybe it's because of you?" she surprised herself with her own words. Andy looked a tad taken aback too. She continued to explain. "If we had not done what we did... I probably would not understand this entirely. I was attracted to you. I have not been attracted to my husband in a very long time. The closeness you and I shared gave me a new perspective. People drift apart, and sometimes what we find with someone else could be what we were missing."

"Is that why you called me here?"

She nodded.

"Reen... I haven't been able to get you off my mind. I know you need time to process your grief and to somehow begin again, but I have gone over this a million times. Our attraction was like nothing I have ever felt before, yes, but it's also you. I want to know you, everything about you. The other night... at the restaurant..." She waited. She wanted him to say more. "When I saw you walk in, I said to my sister that I didn't want to let you go again. If you were back for a reason, I couldn't miss my chance."

They moved closer to each other. He was still touching her. Now that they were past the hard stuff, those words that needed to be said but could have been difficult and uncomfortable, Reen could feel the indescribable closeness with him again. Sure, there were sparks… but it was also as if he could see her soul.

"I didn't want to put your number in my phone. I didn't want to need you."

He smiled a little. "But you do, and it's okay. What do you say we try to find some happiness in our lives again, this time, together?"

Maureen's eyes widened. "What did you just say?"

"That you need me?"

"No, after that."

"Find happiness?"

"Yes," she sighed. She teared up thinking how this was Isaac's wish for her.

"Should we start by drinking coffee?" he suggested, but she saw the sparkle in his eyes.

"The coffee is likely cold by now." Her words were

suggestive, and Andy didn't second guess what she was implying. He stepped closer. He touched the side of her face and he pressed his lips to hers. The attraction was again an out of control inferno. Their kiss deepened. They could not get close enough to each other, standing in that small kitchen.

"Come with me," Maureen was able to say when she came up for air. She could feel his breath on her lips.

They hurried to the only back bedroom in that cottage. He touched her slower this time. He lifted her sweatshirt over her head. She helped him out of his polo shirt. "I want to take my time with you," he spoke softly. "Last time we were on the clock."

She laughed and kissed him hard on the mouth. He pulled her back to look at her. Her breasts were spilling out the top of her black bra. She saw him staring. "Touch me again, Andy. Please." She undid the clasp behind her back and he was there, touching, licking, sucking. She cried out his name and reached for the button on his denim. He pulled off those jeans and boxers while she took off her leggings. He laid her down on the bed and rounded her bottom with the palm of his hand. He then slid off her panties and found her core. He touched her. He put his mouth on her. He didn't stop until she was at his mercy and found her release. And when she did, she looked into his eyes and guided him on top of her body. He entered her slowly and together they found a rhythm that eventually had the old headboard on that bed slamming against the wall. They couldn't stop searching for more of that feeling they brought to each other. And finally, when they found the height of what they were after, they both peaked, released, and fell spent and entangled in each other's arms.

Chapter 19

There was a text and a missed call from Palmer. It was noon before Maureen saw those messages after she and Andy tore themselves away from each other. He went to work, and she stayed at the cottage contemplating her life. Everything was changing and happening so fast. And in typical Maureen fashion, she had doubts and fears.

She called Palmer.

"What could you possibly be so busy doing? I mean, keep your damn phone with you." Palmer was clearly annoyed.

"Please don't tell me that your call was urgent. If something else happened, I don't want to know."

"No. Everything is the same. Listen. Reen, you're by yourself there. The least you can do is stay in touch." Palmer realized how she typically did not overact like that. It was all just too much right now. She especially was worried about knowing that Maureen now had the passcode to Isaac's phone.

"I didn't mean to worry you." Maureen understood why Palmer was upset. "I was busy."

"Doing what?"

Maureen paused. "Can I attach something for you to read in a text right now? It's from the notes in Isaac's phone."

Palmer froze before she responded. "Yes. Right now. I will read it." Palmer was suddenly afraid. "Reen? How bad is it?"

"I just want you to read it. He wrote me a letter, his dad too. I'll send both." Maureen left Palmer on hold for a few minutes. And when she received the text, Palmer started to read the letters.

When she finished reading, Palmer had tears streaming down her face. "Should we have known this?" Maureen could hear the emotion in her voice.

"Some mother I was, huh? No wonder this God of ours took him away from me." This was the raw emotion that surfaced sometimes. It was the cruelty behind grief. One minute, Maureen was doing fine — and the next she was angry and resentful. She worried that her attraction to Andy and the way she had wasted no time to act on those feelings was something she was doing out of spite because she didn't care anymore.

"Stop," Palmer reacted to Maureen's callous words. "You're angry and it's warranted, but this is not your fault."

"I know how he felt," Maureen admitted. "I've told you about myself."

"I wish Isaac had been able to confide in you. And I hate that he knew about Archer's infidelity. Do you blame Archer? I don't want to say this, but what if that was too much for Isaac to process?"

"That could be true. I don't know." Maureen closed her eyes for a moment. "You asked if I blame Archer. A part of me does now, yes. But what good will that do? I'm sure his guilt is eating him alive."

"Have you spoken to him about the letters?"

"I have not shown him the letters, but I will. I sent him the photo that Isaac took from his bedroom window. He captured a moment when his dad was kissing our whore of a neighbor."

"Did Archer defend himself?"

"No. His response was for me to blame him because he certainly blames himself. I ignored his response. I just wanted him to know that I know. I mean, he and Isaac were at odds and I had no idea. I wish I could do it all over again, Palmer. I would have tried so hard to help my boy. I would have been more present."

"Don't. Do not do that to yourself. You were a good mother. I'm not going to listen to you berate yourself."

"I'm human. It will happen. I will rehash and dwell on those what ifs for the rest of my life."

"Isaac said he wanted you to be happy," Palmer noted. "How ironic. I mean, he tried so badly to be whole, and now he's asking you to do it. Consider doing that for him, Reen. You deserve that and so much more."

"I know," she sighed. "I don't want to live out the rest of my life feeling lost or in limbo. It's hard. I feel like two different people right now. My emotions are all over the place. I don't care about anything one minute, and the next I'm questioning my every decision."

"It's called grief. Give yourself some grace. You've lost too much." Palmer didn't have to reiterate how, in addition to Isaac being gone, so was her father, and her marriage was over.

"When I got into town last night, I stopped for some take-out food. I saw Andy dining with another woman." Palmer rolled her eyes, but before she could react, Maureen continued with her story. "I wanted to bolt but he saw me. He came up to me and I discovered that the woman was not his wife, who I suspected, it was his attorney who also happens to be his sister."

"Why is it relevant to know that she's an attorney?"

"She helped him get a divorce. Apparently it can be done even when one party is MIA. It's called divorce by publication." Despite being in the newspaper business, neither one of them had ever heard of it.

"So that means Andy is available," Palmer concluded. "How do you feel about that?"

"I left the restaurant feeling like it was good to see him, as if I was meant to cross paths with him," Maureen admitted. "And then I went to the cottage and settled in for the night."

"You were alone looking at Isaac's phone."

Maureen nodded but Palmer could not see her, so she answered, "Yes."

"I'm sorry you had to go through that pain alone. You should be here. You should be closer. Atta and her dumbass idea to send you away!"

Maureen laughed. "I disagree. This escape is good for me."

"Are you going to call Andy?"

"I did this morning," she confessed. "I woke up feeling vulnerable."

"Uh oh."

Maureen laughed again. "I asked him to come over. I told him about the phone, the letters, all of it. The dam broke. I cried in his arms. I wasn't able to release any emotion last night when I was alone. I can't explain why. Either I was shocked or just numb again. And then the moment he got here this morning, I let go."

"So that's why you were busy when I was trying to get ahold of you?"

Maureen smirked before she spoke. "I told you I was doing something."

"Or someone," Palmer quipped. "You slept with him again, didn't you?"

"I can't explain this. It's easy with him. The attraction is intense. I don't want to think too much, I just want to feel when I am with him."

"Are you using him?" Palmer was direct. No question was too intrusive or off-limits for them.

"I hope not," Maureen's response was honest. "He's a good one. He doesn't deserve another broken heart."

"Is that what you see happening? Is he the one with the greater need?"

"I think we need each other all the same right now."

Palmer accepted that. "Just be careful. You may think this is what you should be doing because it feels good, but what if he's not the happiness you're after?"

"I can't answer that yet."

"Okay. That's understandable."

"Thanks for being supportive. I know my life is a mess, I am a damn mess."

"None of this is your fault. Maybe it's time to start paving a happier path."

"Andy already makes me feel that way. When I am with him, I believe that I deserve all the good things. I feel happy. I also know my Great River Road actions are completely out of character."

"Apparently it's orgasm land."

They both laughed out loud.

"I don't want to hurt him." It was as if Maureen admitted she felt indecisive about her feelings.

"And I don't want to see you get hurt." Palmer knew better than anyone how Maureen had already lived her share of pain and unfairness.

"Then what do I do?" Maureen was serious.

"Live. That's what you should do. If it has to be in the moment right now, so be it. The clarity will come eventually."

Maureen allowed those words to sink in. "That might be the most sense you've ever made."

Chapter 20

She was invited to dinner. She told him yes. Afterward, Maureen second guessed herself. Could she really go to Andy's house and have dinner with him and Joey, mimicking as if they were a family? She had a family once — but not anymore. Her son was gone, her marriage had unraveled. Was she trying too hard, too fast to replace what she lost? Would she only be leading them on by forcing something fictional to be a reality? Or was this something she really wanted? Could the two of them be her future? She told herself that she was overthinking. Then she got ready and left.

The door swung open, and Joey's smile met his eyes. "Reen! My dad just said you don't have to ring our doorbell. You're not a guest anymore."

"No?" Maureen spoke in response to not being a guest. "What am I then?' she teased.

Joey shrugged his small shoulders. "Well, you're my friend, but I think my dad likes you like a girl."

Maureen laughed out loud. Given the things she had already done with his dad, Maureen agreed, *Andy liked her like a girl.*

She looked up and saw Andy leaning against the open doorway that led into the kitchen. He smiled at her, and gosh did that smile ever meet his eyes, too. She felt internally tingly from the newness of him. She questioned if she had ever felt that way with Archer. Did she once experience that dizzy-headed, heart-pounding, head-over-heels emotion? Or had Archer just felt safe because at that time in her life she was ready for a husband and a family of her own?

"I hope you're hungry," he spoke first.

"I am, but I hope you two didn't go through too much trouble for me." She already saw the pizza box on the table behind him.

He chuckled when he saw her looking. "Pizza and wings. Only the best for our new friend."

This time her smile ignited a sparkle in her eyes.

The dinner conversation was effortless, the laughter was genuine, and Maureen was truly having a good time with them. Afterward, she offered to help clear the table, but Joey pulled her by the hand. He wanted to show her his swing in the backyard.

Andy suggested for the two of them to go out and he would join them after he loaded the dishwasher.

There were dark clouds in the sky when Maureen and Joey stepped onto the patio. "Looks like it's going to rain," she noted, as she held her half-full wine glass from dinner, and Joey ran through the backyard to the tree line. As Maureen followed him, she was focused solely on that swing. The one Joey was excited to show her. It was a tire swing with a heavy rope. It was a braided polypropylene rope. It was thick and had a natural brown color. Maureen could feel her heart rate increase when Joey pulled himself up on the tire and reached for two of the three lengths of rope that were looped over the branch above and tied around the tire below. Her eyes scanned that rope from top to bottom, and all over again. She saw the loops. Her mind flashed to the noose. The one in her son's bedroom. In the closet. It was the same type of rope, and that awful scene was playing out, over and over again, in flashbacks, in her mind.

Maureen dropped her wine glass on the ground at her feet. The red wine splashed all over the blades of grass and on her white tennis shoes. A loud crack of thunder boomed in the sky. Joey was startled. Maureen was numb. And Andy was walking swiftly through the backyard now.

She heard his voice carry. He said something to her, or to Joey, but she couldn't make out the words. She never turned around. The scene on replay in her mind had taken her somewhere else. Some place as dark as the sky above. The thunder suddenly brought on rain. A downpour of hard drops were pounding from the sky. She never saw Joey hop off the swing and run to her. She never felt his hand tugging on hers to get her to move. She only dropped to her knees, holding her head in her hands while she cried. Andy reached her quickly. He tried to pull her to her feet, but she was like a deadweight. Her eyes were distant, as if she were in a trance.

"Reen? You okay? Can you hear me?"

"What's going on, dad? What's wrong with Reen?"

Andy dropped to his knees, right where the wine had spilled, and the stemless glass was tipped on its side amid long blades of grass.

"It's okay, Reen. Talk to me. I can help." Joey stood close, his full height now reaching his father's shoulder. The rain soaked all of them. Even so, they could still make out the tears streaming down her face.

"The, the ro- the ro- pe," she tried to speak through her tears. And suddenly she realized Joey was too close. She couldn't traumatize him like that. She was no good for him, or for his father. She was a messed up, scarred soul, who would forever be triggered by what life had so unfairly thrown at her. She had taken one look at a tire swing and lost herself in the trauma all over again.

She unsteadily forced herself to her feet. Andy was right there, attempting to help her. "I have go," she told him.

"No. Not like this. It's raining too hard. We all need to go inside and be safe."

"No," she backed away and started to run through the yard, with the intention of making her way around to the front of the house, to the driveway where her car was parked.

Andy reached for Joey and told him to go inside and take cover while he took care of Reen. He then ran after her. She only made it to the driver's side but not inside the car. That's when it occurred to her that her purse, her phone, and her car keys were still inside the house.

She turned her body around, pressed it against the closed car door, and slid down until her bottom reached the concrete. She sobbed at how defeated she felt. A few seconds later, Andy got to her.

"Talk to me." The rain was pounding them. He was spitting it from his lips as he spoke.

"I am no good for you two," she cried.

"That's not true," he objected. "I want to know what happened to you out there."

"My son," was all she managed to say. "In his closet. That day." Andy listened raptly. "He used a rope… just like that one." She bent forward, put her face in her hands, and openly wailed.

Andy's heart sunk. He pulled her close, and he held onto her for dear life as he enveloped her in his strong arms with everything he had. He was not about to let her go. Now or ever.

"I am so sorry. I can't change what happened," he was searching for the right words. "But I can be here for you. I can show you. I will prove to you that you can count on me for the good and the awful. And, Reen, I know what you went through was unbelievably awful. Let me help you through the pain. Please. I want to help you."

"I'm so broken," she tried to convince him to back away as she pried herself from his arms. "I need to go. I need time. Please, go inside and get my things. I can't face Joey like this. I have already scared him. What kind of person loses control like that in front of a child?"

"I will explain to him that you lost your boy. I don't have to tell him how. I will just tell him that you're sad and you're going to be sad for a lifetime. But I will also help him understand that life is hard and in order to power through the pain, we need each other."

"Andy, I can't. I'm not ready."

He didn't question what she meant by those words. He only hoped in this moment she was not ready to go back inside and carry on with what began as a fun evening.

"I want you to understand something before I let you go home tonight. I will go get your things, but first you have to listen, you have to hear me."

She nodded.

"Allow yourself some mercy. I want you to think about all we could have together. You don't have to find closure for anything that happened to you before us. I will help you carry the weight. No one's life is put together neatly. You know my story." He was blinking back the rain from his eyes. He stared at her. The way she looked now reminded him exactly of the day he first met her when he fished her out of the river. My God, he loved her. He had fallen in love with her the moment he saw her, touched her, spoke to her. "This is real life. Lives are sloppy, relationships are messy. Our stories before were poorly written, they ended too early or maybe too late, I don't know which. What I know for sure is this, what you and I have, feels like a brand-new chapter that I cannot wait to watch unfold for the rest of my life." He looked at her, but her face was difficult to read. "I don't want to freak you out. This isn't what I do. I don't feel things like this. Something happened when you came into my life, and Joey's. You slammed into our hearts. I know, for me, it was as if you sent my wrecked world plummeting into that river that I pulled you out of. You make me better, and I don't want to ever turn away from something like that." He was afraid if he confessed his love for her, she would bolt, so he kept those words tucked inside his heart. For now.

"I don't deserve you," was all she said. "I need to go. Please."

Andy stalled, remaining on his knees on the puddled ground in front of her. "Can I call you to check on you later?" She didn't respond. "At least let me know when you make it back to the cottage."

She nodded.

He stood. He ran through the sideways rainfall, toward the house. When he returned, he used the key remote to unlock her car. She got to her feet, and he guided her soaked-self inside the vehicle.

"Thank you," she said to him, and then paused before she added, "I'm sorry, Andy."

He shook his head as if he refused to allow those words to mean anything close to a goodbye. "It's alright. Be safe driving."

He watched her back down his driveway. He stood there letting the rain drench him some more. What did it matter, he was already wet. And when she drove off, he walked inside the house. He stood on the welcome mat right in front of the door in the foyer. Joey was right there the moment he came back. He had been staring out the window, watching them the entire time.

"Is she gone dad? Is she never coming back, like mom?"

Andy reached for his son's face. He held his cheeks in his cold, wet hands, and he looked directly into his sad eyes. "No, son. She needs us, and we are going to be there for her when she's ready. We will try our hardest to make her feel loved."

Joey choked back his tears, and asked, "You love her too, dad?"

"I sure do," Andy sighed, and Joey's little face broke into a smile.

Chapter 21

Three days passed. Maureen had been in touch with Palmer. She knew what happened. She was worried about her. She threatened to go there and drag her back home. That's when Maureen reminded her that she did not have a home of her own. For now, she wanted that place to be the cottage. Still, Palmer was worried sick. Enough to go to someone else for help.

Atta invited Palmer to sit down at the kitchen table. The weather had turned wintry so sitting in those rocking chairs on the wraparound front porch would have to wait a while.

Palmer was careful to sip the hot coffee in the mug that Atta placed on the table in front of her.

"Are you hungry?" Atta asked her, because that's what a mother did.

She shook her head. "I need you to hear me. There's a lot going on with Reen, and I don't know if I can reach her anymore."

"Is she still at the cottage?" Atta's voice was calm. The woman never panicked. Even when Palmer told her parents that Isaac had died, her father wailed, and her mother had only dropped her head and closed her eyes. She processed everything quietly. Sometimes, however, holding in the pain took a wrong turn. Palmer still could not believe her mother lost her head all those years ago when she sought revenge on the woman who slept with her man. Atta still did not know that Palmer knew her secret.

"She doesn't want to leave there," Palmer told her. "She met someone. A man and his son have stolen her heart. I want to believe they are good for her, she seemed happy or more carefree whenever she spoke of them. She's not ready though, or she feels undeserving of finding happiness so soon after she lost Isaac. I don't know. She was triggered recently when she saw a tire swing in the backyard of their house. It had a similar rope that

Isaac used…"

"Oh, dear God," Atta reacted.

"She hasn't been the same since. She's hardly present during my calls, and she's not responding to Andy and Joey, that's the man and his son who live near Great River Road."

"She needs time," Atta defended Maureen.

"Time for what? Time to regress and lose herself further? I disagree about giving her space or letting too much time pass. Not much has changed in the last four decades. Reen is still broken and vulnerable and she needs us."

"You said as much when you were nine years old and brought her here for the first time after school."

"I need your help to save her again, mom."

Atta patted her daughter's hand on the table. "You must understand that being triggered isn't something she can control," Atta began to explain, as if she, too, knew it well. "It happens automatically and instantly if something feels familiar to a previous trauma. Your physiology will move you into a state of fight, flight, or freeze. It's not her fault she cannot talk herself out of it or change it."

"You sound as if you are speaking from experience," Palmer noted.

"You act as if you do not know," Atta called her out. "Don't think for a second that I don't know that you know."

Palmer laughed a little at her word usage. "Reen and I share everything."

"I'm well aware. I guess you could say I used that to my advantage. It was easier to tell you what I did through Reen. I didn't want to see the disappointment in your eyes."

Palmer shook her head. "It was more like shock. And for what it's worth, dad was to blame, too. What he did pushed you past your limit."

"That was a long time ago."

"It's a part of your story," Palmer noted. "So, will you try to reach Reen?'

"Of course, I will," Atta paused, her hoarse voice suddenly forced her to cough. "But I think she already knows that we are all a moment away from becoming a totally different person. What I mean is… life happens. A car crash, a diagnosis, an unexpected phone call, or something wonderful —like a newfound love— can change everything.

"Tell her that," was all Palmer said. And after her daughter left the farmhouse, Atta knew exactly what she would do to help Maureen.

Chapter 22

The air was chilly, but Maureen was bundled up and walking through the leaves on the grounds of her cottage. They should have been raked a month ago, and now she considered going into town to buy a rake to keep herself busy and active. Andy had been trying so hard to get her to open up to him again. He sent daily uplifting messages. He wanted her to know that he cared, that he and Joey both missed her. Maureen knew it was only a matter of time before he drove to her cottage. He wasn't demanding or obsessive, but he was a man who didn't give up very easily. Maureen, on the other hand, had given up on everything. These days she felt as numb as she did on the day she buried her son. It was just easier not to feel anything.

She looked up from the yard when she heard a vehicle coming up the rock road, toward her cottage. She looked twice when she saw Jon Boy's old farm truck that was once cherry red, but the sun had faded it and the weather had rusted it year after year.

Her eyes widened when she saw Atta behind the wheel. She was eighty-something years old, and she drove herself an hour away from home. Already, Maureen knew she was going to have her hands full with her being there. Fortunately, she had made it there in one piece, but Maureen would be the one to get her back home safely. First, she walked toward the truck to see what brought her all that way.

She killed the engine that blew exhaust or something that smelled as if it was running rich. Maureen held in a cough as the driver's side door flew open. "Don't look at me as if you are surprised I've got a sense of direction. I have this phone with me that you girls gave to me last Christmas, I found the map thingee, and this nice lady talked to me the whole way here. I mean, she even navigated me through Highland, where I know every turn and what's on every corner."

Maureen laughed out loud and took her hand as she slid her bony bottom off the front bench seat that was torn and tattered in at least three places.

Atta's Uggs met the rock ground, and Maureen advised her to pick up her feet when she walked and not slide them.

"Can we go inside?" Atta asked. "The air is just too cold for me lately."

"I will take you inside," Maureen told her, "and then you are going to tell me why in the world you came all this way."

Atta declined anything to eat or drink. She only took off her coat, asked where the bathroom was to relieve her bladder, and then she returned to the living room to sit down on the sofa. Maureen covered her legs with her and Isaac's favorite blanket.

"I'm comfortable, thank you," Atta responded.

"Good. Now talk to me. I find it very hard to believe that Palmer sent you. If she did, she has lost her mind, too."

"Is that the way you feel? As if you're making mindless decisions?" Atta put her on the spot. "Have you succumbed to the pain and given up on everything and everyone?"

Maureen stared at her. "I would never give up on you or Palmer. You're my family."

"Right," Atta agreed. "People come and go, but once in a while you meet certain ones who you know are going to stay in your life forever. But what about the ones who unexpectedly arrive to shake things up, to show you true love, and force you to see yourself like no one else ever has?"

"Are you speaking from your experience, the one you shared with me from long ago?" Maureen directed this conversation subject back to Atta.

"It didn't matter to me where he came from or why he came," Atta began to talk about her own story again. "All that really mattered to me was how he made me feel. I laughed more when he was around. I began to notice my smile. There was a new light in my eyes. I discovered things about myself I had never known before. My time with him was only meant to be temporary, but it was indeed life changing."

"Do you regret never seeing him again?"

Atta shook her head. "He was young, much younger than I. I've imagined him to have lived a very full life, just as he deserved." She paused before she spoke some more. "And, no, I do not carry regret. The years spent with my Jon was where I belonged."

"I've met someone," Maureen cautiously began, but somehow saying those words out loud to anyone else except for Palmer had made it seem more real, and also more terrifying.

"Quinn filled me in." Atta used her birth-given name.

Maureen didn't react.

"You know your own heart," Atta continued. "I am only going to remind you of how I have lived ever since my own experience with someone who came out of nowhere and left an imprint on my soul."

"We're not going to talk about the hot sex, are we?" Maureen tried to be lighthearted, and it made her giggle to think of how Palmer would react if she were there. This was her mother. It was different for Maureen. Easier, actually, in some ways.

"Don't think I'm too old to relive those times in my memory." Atta winked at her, and Maureen laughed out loud.

Atta grew serious again.

"I just want you to realize what is right in front of you. I don't have to preach to you about life being fleeting. You will always reel from your son being taken away from you in an instant. I won't tell you to appreciate what you have before it's gone, because you have lost too much in your forty-eight years of life. But, what I want to do is ask you to focus on yourself. Be selfish. What if there were only ten more summers, or fifty more sunrises in your life? What if you have already read your favorite book, traveled for the last time, or only have three more times to tell someone that you love them? Wouldn't that change things? It should. Nothing is forever. Even I thought my Jon and I would still be holding hands for another decade. Live for today, my dear Reen. Give yourself everything. Allow yourself to be happy."

There were tears in Maureen's eyes.

"You think I should go to them." She referred to Andy and his son. She already loved them both so much.

"You hold the answer to your own question. What do you want to do with the rest of your life?"

Maureen carefully removed the blanket from Atta's legs, and then she stood up and neatly folded it in half. "Come on, I'm going to drive you home in my car. We will worry about Jon Boy's beat up farm truck some other day."

Atta stood up. "And then what?"

"And then I want to go see my son at his final resting place."

"He's not really there, you know."

"It's still his marker, that stone will be what is left to prove his existence for eternity."

"What will you tell him?"

Maureen swallowed the lump rising in her throat. "That I forgive him for giving up on himself."

Atta reached for her hand to comfort the daughter who was born in her heart the moment she met her as a little girl.

"I've never told you what to do. I have only tried to guide you." Maureen silently agreed. "I do think your next stop should be to see Archer. Be sure he knows he's not to blame."

Again, Maureen silently agreed.

"And, from there where should I go?'

"Come back here to this quaint little cottage and take it from there. I don't think you need me, or anyone else, to tell you where to look for your happiness. You've already found it all on your own. Now it's time for you to live it."

Chapter 23

Atta was safe and sound, back at the farmhouse, when Maureen drove to the cemetery. She had not been there since the day of her son's funeral. She had not been able to return to that mound of dirt on the ground with the temporary laminated piece of paper that read, Isaac J. Ryan, with his birth date and death date, separate by a dash. How unfair that the dash had symbolized very little time in between. Fourteen years of life and then he was gone too soon.

Maureen stared at the ground, all the freshly moved dirt, and the flowers. There were so many flowers. She wanted nothing to do with bringing those back to the house. All she said to the funeral director was 'please bring them to the cemetery and leave them there.'

She stood with her arms crossed over her chest. The air temperature felt a little less chilly now than it had earlier today at the cottage. She noticed again that the clouds in the sky were darkening, and she believed that fit her mood. It was a dark time for any mother to stand on the cemetery grounds at her own child's gravesite. She wanted to lash out at the universe, or the God that her adoptive parents tried to get her to believe in as a child, a teenager, and later an adult. But Maureen knew the true root of her anger was for her son. Isaac not only took his own life, but he robbed her of so much as well. Because he was gone, she would never have a daughter-in-law, and she would never be a grandma.

"I wish you had talked to me. I could have gotten you some help. You took the coward's way out, Isaac Ryan." Maureen was aware she had raised her voice. "I am so angry and so sad and so unbelievably grateful that you were my son, if only for a short time. You were something. I want you to know that. I was so proud. Did I tell you that enough? You were my son and I loved you with all my heart. I still do. I always will. I understand that you felt lost, I do. I promise you, I am able to comprehend that, just like when a heart stops beating, your sense of reason was lost in your brain at the end. You believed what you were about to do was the only way out. Well, you were wrong. There's always hope. There's always a light in the darkness, somewhere.

Sometimes we just have to look harder. I know I will now. Isaac, I promise you I will find the light. For the rest of my life, I will honor your memory in that way."

There were raindrops falling from the sky now. Maureen looked up. "What is with the fucking rain again!" Following that outburst, she laughed out loud. "It's you, isn't it? It was you at the tire swing, and it's you again now." She smiled up at the dark sky, tasting the raindrops on her lips.

And then she watched a vehicle drive up the lane road in the middle of the cemetery and it parked behind hers. It would be silly for her to wonder what the chances were for Archer to show up there. Isaac was his son, too.

He pulled the hood of his rain jacket over his head and walked up to her. "I was driving by..." was all he said, and Maureen stayed silent. "I wish I had an umbrella with me to offer you." The rain beat down harder as he spoke.

Maureen looked up at him now. "I was never much for using an umbrella. I'll take the rain, I'll let it drench me until it decides it's had enough. It's symbolic, isn't it? Life likes to beat me down like the damn rain falling from the sky right now."

"I'm sorry," were the only words that Archer could muster to say to her.

"Me, too," she responded. "I'm sorry that we screwed up as parents, I'm sorry that we didn't love each other enough to make our marriage last. And, I'm sorry that we both have to grieve for our son for the rest of our lives. Because, given everything, we don't deserve that kind of pain."

Archer looked surprised by her words. The downpour suddenly stopped as the two of them stood there together in shared silence. Maureen had said enough, and Archer was unsure how to respond.

But finally, he asked her, "You don't blame me?"

She shook her head and reached into her coat pocket for her phone. "He wrote us both letters. I want you to read them." Archer took her phone into his hand and began to read. First, he read the letter meant for him. And finally, there were tears streaming down his face when he finished both letters.

"He was so angry with me."

"Yet, he loved you. Hold onto what he said when he signed off. He loved you," she repeated.

"He clearly loved you more."

"I won't argue with that," she smirked.

"You never disappointed him."

"Yes, I did. We both did. We were never enough. Could we have done it better? Yes, but that doesn't matter now. What matters is how much we loved him, and we know he loved us back. Archer," she caught his full attention before she continued, "we are not to blame. He is."

"How do we forgive him for that?" Archer was fighting back the tears again.

"I think I already have. I mean, I have to in order to live again. He took so much from us that day... we can't let him take any more. I want to be happy and whole, Archer. And, you should be, too."

"How did you get to this point?" He didn't want to say it, but she had been numb and completely detached. Even before their son died, she was broken.

"I am not entirely there," she admitted, "but I want to be."

A part of him wanted to tell her that he would help her, that they could try again and help each other to heal. But he knew better. They weren't meant to be. Just as their son was not meant to grow up, grow old, and one day outlive his parents.

The sun peered from behind the clouds. Archer reached for her hand. For now, she was still his wife. Maureen grabbed ahold of him one last time, because she wanted to show her son that forgiveness was freeing. If only Isaac had understood that the sky's darkness was only temporary.

Chapter 24

The trip back to Great River Road did not lead her directly to the cottage this time. She didn't allow herself to second guess her decision to drive straight to that firetruck red house near the riverbank. She only hoped she was not too late. Would they still want her, broken and all?

There was only one way for her to know.

She rang the doorbell and stepped back from the entrance.

This time she did not hear little feet running through the house, pounding the hardwood flooring that led to the door. She waited. She debated ringing the bell again. And finally, she turned away.

She took a few steps on the driveway when she heard a voice behind her.

"Reen?'

It was Andy. He was walking around the side of the house, coming from the backyard. Her last memory of that backyard was hardly a pleasant one.

"Hi," she said to him.

"I'm glad you came by. I saw the ring doorbell notification on my phone. I was just in the backyard, picking up some toys that Joey left out."

"Is Joey home?"

"No. He's at basketball practice."

"I'm sorry I missed him."

"You can come see him anytime, Reen. We both want you here as often as you want to be."

"Even after the episode in the rain last time?" A part of her was embarrassed, but she also knew what happened was out of her control. Her trauma was the kind that delved deep. She only hoped she was strong enough to overcome it now, and for the rest of her life.

"Especially so," Andy answered her. "We want to help you. Joey has been so concerned. He's asked a lot of questions. Maybe you could help him understand things sometime?"

"That boy," she sighed, "I love him so much."

Andy stared for a moment. "He loves you, too."

She felt her heart swell. Were they still talking about Joey? Or were they standing on his driveway, at least ten feet apart, confessing their own feelings for each other?

"How does something so deep and so true happen so suddenly?" Maureen meant falling in love.

"I don't think we should try to explain it or somehow define it," Andy suggested. "Instead, let's just savor it."

"Are we still talking about Joey?" she teased him a little, but she needed to know more.

Andy smiled that smile, the one that met his eyes every single time. He was the most genuine human being she had ever laid eyes on... and touched... and had fallen for beyond words.

"My son adores you. I know that without a doubt," Andy confidently stated. "His father, however, has fallen so madly in love with you that he cannot eat, sleep, or breathe without having you near him."

She inhaled. She loved him so.

"Is this close enough?" Maureen signaled the space that remained between them on the driveway.

"Almost."

She took three steps closer to him.

"How's this?"

He chuckled under his breath.

She moved in closer to him.

Close enough for him to be able to reach out his arms to her.

She reached back for him.

They clasped hands.

He reeled her as close to him as she could possibly be. She was in his arms. She felt his pulse as her own.

"This," he said, "is where you belong."

She felt those words in her soul. *She belonged.*

About the Author

This story involved one of the most sensitive topics I've ever written about. Losing a child in any way has to be the most unbearable pain and grief. Knowing a child has taken his or her own life adds an entirely new dimension to that suffering. *Almost*, my 39th novel, focuses on a mother who is forced to face that her teenage son is gone and she has absolutely no idea why he ended his life. There is a harsh reality in this storyline, knowing some people must face the fact that they never will find out the reason why.

How do you go on?

How does anyone find happiness when the triggers from the trauma continue to loom in their lives, night and day? Oddly, sometimes life will completely break us down, and in that brokenness, we will find ourselves.

Maureen, the heroine in this story, eventually discovers that she and her son shared a similar pain. *Almost* was a complicated, out of reach, word for them. Almost home… Almost happy… Almost feeling as if they belonged. Almost, but not quite.

This is a story of discovery and acceptance, and the realization that we have to make our own happiness. It's up to us how big a bite we want to take out of life.

As always, thank you for reading!

love,

Lori Bell

Made in the USA
Monee, IL
23 September 2024

66365325R00120